THE KNIGHT'S ORDER

Found a typo? Oh no! Every book has at least one typo and we want to make our book as perfect as possible.

Let us know at www. JAAlexsoo.com/contact-me

If you want exclusive content, behind the scene adventures, information about J.A. Alexsoo's next novel, or other topics for readers and fantasy fans, you can sign up for her newsletter. Your email will remain confidential and you can unsubscribe anytime.

Visit: www. JAAlexsoo.com

We'd love to know your thoughts!

Please leave a review for *The Knight's Order* on

AMAZON

or

www. goodreads.com

We can't wait to hear your feedback!

THE KNIGHT'S ORDER

J·A· ALEXSOO

Library and Archives Canada Cataloguing in Publication

Alexsoo, J. A., author

    The knight's order / J.A. Alexsoo.

(Knights of Mythreth ; book 1)

Issued in print and electronic formats.

ISBN 978-0-9952378-0-3 (paperback).--ISBN 978-0-9952378-3-4 (EPUB)

    I. Title.

PS8601.L36K65 2016   C813'.6   C2016-905851-4

                                C2016-905852-2

First Printing October 2016

Cover by Hugh Pindur

Editing by David Antrobus

Published by Breezy Pages Publishing

WWW.JAALEXSOO.COM

To Nan, my biggest fan,
your enthusiasm carried me through this journey.
Thank you, with all my heart.

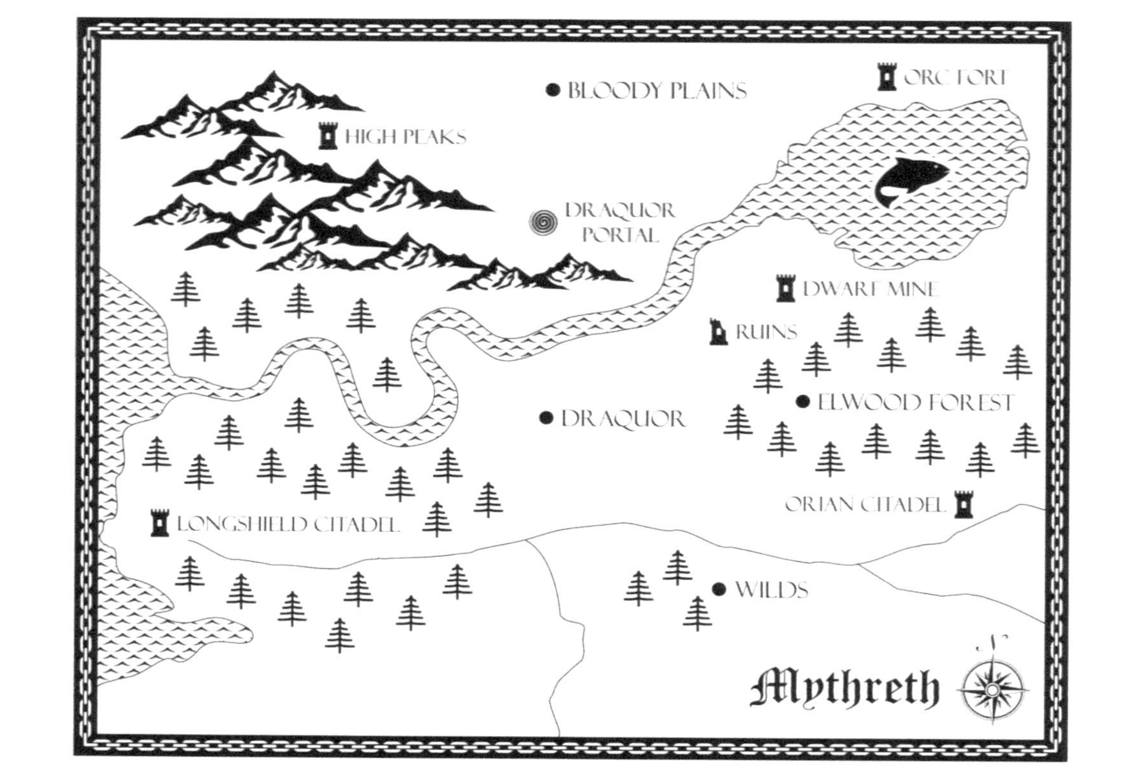
BLOODY PLAINS
ORC FORT
HIGH PEAKS
DRAQUOR PORTAL
DWARF MINE
RUINS
ELWOOD FOREST
DRAQUOR
ORIAN CITADEL
LONGSHIELD CITADEL
WILDS
Mythreth

PROLOGUE

W e could split up, to cover more ground."

Guardian Brant Cormell considered the words. Someone who'd spent less time with the lad would've thought his suggestion was born from his eagerness to return to the citadel, where a warm meal and a soft bed awaited him. Cormell knew better. As members of the Avant Guard Order, it was their duty to keep peace in the lands, and the boy wasn't one to pass up the chance for adventure.

Boy. It was a description that no longer fit his trainee. Aden was well on his way to becoming a knight, and Cormell knew that the time was soon approaching. Aden had grown into a bright and strong young man, one who'd do great things for the world.

Cormell nodded as he judged how much time they had. "Better to investigate before we lose the light."

Aden hurried off to scout the area, eagerly searching for any clues as to where the attackers had gone. Cormell watched his trainee fade into the shadows of the evening, but his thoughts remained on the situation they'd come across. He stood on the main road that climbed a small hill, giving him a view of the surrounding forest. In the distance, the city of Avender surrounded Longshield Citadel that towered over it. With the day soon over, small lights of civilization began twinkling like beacons calling them home. They couldn't return, however, not until they uncovered what had killed the men here.

City guards frequently patrolled the main road that led to Avender. The unusual behavior of one such patrol had caught their attention as he and Aden Fendrie, his knight in training, were returning from their latest mission. While flying above on their wyvernkin mounts, they'd discovered the troubling scene below. They had cautiously approached on foot; landing in the midst of a potential trap was never wise, and they were keenly aware that the forest offered ample cover. As they drew near, there was no sign of immediate danger.

Cormell surveyed the area thoroughly, taking care to catch every detail. The victims lay still and lifeless on the ground, while their lit torches were scattered around them. Dry branches littered the road and had caught on fire; an old abandoned cart was ablaze at the side of the path. The flames made the old wood crack and groan in protest, while the smell of smoke permeated the air. From the state of things, it was apparent that the authorities responsible for keeping the road clean had become too lax in their duties. Cormell knelt and inspected the nearest corpse. The man's throat had been cleanly cut, and his sword still lay sheathed in its scabbard.

After taking a moment to scan the other bodies, he deduced that they'd been taken by surprise and killed proficiently by a skilled hand.

An uneasy feeling crept over him as he studied where the men had fallen, and their wounds. The number of guards was strange as well. *Don't road patrols usually consist of only four... and where's their missing gear...?*

"Was it really necessary to kill them?" Cormell spoke, unsure where to direct his words.

A guttural chuckle swelled from an impostor, the one who'd been lying near a wheel of the cart. The figure rose, adorned with various pieces of armor from his victims. He appeared as any patrol guard, even using blood to complete the illusion. He stripped off the plated protection to reveal the minimal leathers beneath, most covering his upper chest. Cormell spotted a few small knives throughout the scant armor but knew there were plenty more strategically hidden. Preferring to be barefoot, the man kicked off the cumbersome boots and replaced the helmet with a wide-brimmed hat. "I wanted to grab your attention."

"Well, you've got it! Why did you murder these men? What are you after?"

The stranger grinned beneath his hat, but his eyes remained hidden. "Your life."

The Order made many enemies of the brigands across the lands, so the words didn't surprise Cormell. What made his pulse race was the distinct yet subtle smell that he detected. "So... how does a goblin profit from my death?"

The creature paused. The dark eyes that studied him

changed to a deep red. "Was I that obvious?"

Cormell then witnessed what few had observed: what appeared to be a human man change into something he'd seen only once before. Like his past encounter, the creature's skin turned a deep green, and his nails grew sharp and black. His face scrunched in a permanent glare, while his nose became short, flat, and wide. Thin lips pursed together above an elongated chin. Lean muscles tightened throughout the body, and his limbs remained slightly bent, as if ready to pounce at any moment. His stature shortened, and his cut trousers became full-length pants as he was now two-thirds the height of an average man. Despite the goblin's size, Cormell knew better than to underestimate him, understanding all too well the strength and agility of the creature.

Goblins were a reclusive race, able to take on the forms of other species when they devoured the heart of their prey. Those that ventured into societies preferred to hide behind an intellectual mask rather than the animal kind of their brethren in the wilds. Most that chose to live in societies preferred and excelled at mercenary work, greatly benefiting from their ability to change appearance.

In Cormell's experience, goblins were more common than people thought. Most were either ignorant of their brush with fate or died from the confrontation. He'd been fortunate so far, and could identify the smell that gave them away, but he didn't reveal these specifics to the creature. "I've had my share of encounters with your kind, and I've learned of some names that might interest you."

He traced the names in the air with a finger, using magic to keep the letters in place. He slowly retrieved a blank parchment from his pocket and bound the words to it. He was tempted to grab his verge stone to warn Aden of the danger, but the goblin scrutinized his every move. From the caustic look in the creature's eyes, he knew it would be a mistake. So instead, he tossed the parchment, which was deftly caught by his adversary.

Goblins were a sub-demonic race. To learn their names was to have power over them. That was why most of them feared the Avant Guard Order, since their members were of the few who could learn such secretive information. In goblin culture, it was a disgrace, and their brethren would kill them for it.

This wasn't why Cormell now shared what he knew with this creature, who opened the paper with interest. It was to serve as a distraction as he readied a covert attack of his own. Before he did, he wanted to warn his trainee, but it was impossible without his verge stone in hand. He had to defeat the goblin quickly, before Aden returned. Cormell was afraid for the boy who had no experience with these crafty and dangerous creatures.

"Ah, this name is familiar. He was always a fool, I'll enjoy hunting him," the goblin said with amusement.

Cormell sucked in a breath, unwilling to waste this opportunity while the creature was preoccupied. The magic tingled through him as he concentrated on the goblin's mental defenses. He managed to strike three times before the creature held up a hand, palm outward, as if to physically stop the attack.

"Enough." The word held its own power and deflected the magic. The creature's defenses remained unscathed, crushing Cormell's hopes of a quick battle. The goblin calmly slid the parchment into a pouch on his belt. "Well, back to business then. You may have been lucky in the past, but not today."

Cormell's hand instinctively went to the hilt of his sword, then paused when he caught a glimpse of his trainee. Aden had circled behind the creature and crept quietly toward him.

"Get away! He's a goblin!" Cormell waved in warning.

"What—?" Aden began, but as his foot touched the ground he triggered a well-placed trap.

The creature instantly attacked Cormell, and he narrowly deflected the vicious assault. The daggers pressed firmly against his sword, and the goblin mocked him with a thin-lipped smirk. Cormell glanced in Aden's direction but received a hard kick in the abdomen for his efforts. He staggered back from the blow as he heard a cry of pain. He ignored his throbbing midsection and immediately searched for Aden again, and saw the boy standing on a glowing emerald rune. The air shimmered with the same green magic, and two eel-like creatures occupied the space with the trainee. The eels remained suspended in the air, as though they were under water. One had its teeth deep in Aden's thigh, while the other had the boy's forearm in its jaws and slowly drained their victim's energy and power. Magic held the trainee in place, while bolts of electricity surged through the air and occasionally shocked him.

All this happened within moments, and Cormell knew they had little time now. His attention returned to the goblin, who seemed to sense his desperation and taunted him with a wicked grin.

"You want to save your pupil? Better hurry, few survive containment for long."

Cormell heard Aden call to him but remained focused on his formidable enemy. He grabbed his cloak and threw it around his shoulders. The goblin's eyes widened when the fabric fell to the ground, and he was nowhere to be found. Cormell slashed at him from behind, but his adversary instinctively dodged it with a dive-and-roll. When the creature regained his feet, he immediately turned and sent a knife flying at Cormell, who easily deflected it but was pressured to keep moving as more knives followed. He knocked the last blade away and saw the goblin circle him. Cormell blocked the dagger thrusts, and the clash of their blades rang through the air. They exchanged blow for blow, their battle evolving into a deadly dance of swordsmanship.

The air temperature became biting cold where Cormell fired his magic. The creature sneered and pushed away and barely avoided the explosions of the frost traps.

Once the goblin was clear of the danger, he skidded to a stop. "Ice? Really? You can do better."

"Yes, I can."

The creature tried to spin away but was already ensnared in Cormell's magic. Golden tendrils of light snaked up from a nearby rune on the ground, wrapping around their target. They forced their captive to kneel, and while holding him in place, squeezed his wrists so tight that he dropped his weapons. The goblin wrestled with his bindings, but to no avail. The tip of Cormell's blade then rested at his throat.

"Release him, now."

It was only Cormell's principles and duty as a knight that held him back from killing the goblin outright. Aside from that, there was no guarantee that the magic holding Aden would release him once the creature was dead. It was a risk he wouldn't take since his trainee had been confined for too long already. If the goblin refused, he'd do what he must.

"As you wish."

The magic vanished, the eels released their victim, and Aden crumbled to the ground. Cormell feared he'd been too late until the boy struggled to his feet. He was breathing hard, clearly in pain and disoriented from the assaults. Despite that, he kept moving toward his guardian.

Cormell relaxed slightly, and even the goblin seemed intrigued.

"Your pupil is hardier than expected. He made it through the ordeal, but... you should have killed me when you had the chance."

There was a sudden flash of light and a sound like the shattering of glass. Cormell was taken off guard as his magic was neutralized so effectively, something he'd never encountered before. He knew goblins to be intelligent and devious, but he was unaware that they had such power. He thrust his sword forward, but now free of his bonds the creature used his forearm to divert Cormell's blade off its mark. The goblin closed in, and Cormell felt the force of the knife's impact as it stabbed his abdomen, followed by a sharp explosion of agony.

"Don't worry," the creature snickered, "I didn't hit anything vital. I want you alive a little longer."

The goblin retracted the blade, and Cormell immediately covered the wound with his hand. The creature stepped away, then turned back to study him. "You're cleverer than most"— his smile held no mirth as green fire engulfed one of his hands and his spell built in power— "but now your pupil will die."

The creature hurled the magic in Aden's direction and released the spell just as Cormell's sword sliced through his limb. Cormell heard the scream of the creature behind him, but lost his grip on the blade in his haste. There was no time to retrieve it as the world seemed to slow and the fire careened straight for his trainee. Cormell cast a short transpo spell and appeared ahead of the deadly magic. He stood in its path, determined to protect the boy behind him. He managed to get a quick glimpse of Aden, who'd collapsed but was still crawling forward.

Cormell turned to face the approaching inferno. As the flames connected with his barrier, a thought crossed his mind: *This was his plan all along.* The goblin had been building the spell for some time, the sheer size and power of the fire a testament to the fact.

The magic slammed against his will, and he defiantly pushed back. He clenched his jaw from the exertion, feeling on the verge of being consumed. He put all his strength behind blocking the fiery mass. A noise escaped him, an agonizing roar that fueled him. With one last surge of power he tore the magic apart.

As the blaze dissipated and Cormell took in a breath of

relief, something struck him in the left shoulder and he staggered back from the force. He looked up at the goblin, who was gripping his bloody stump where his hand had been. Cormell's sword was secured on his belt. The creature's chest rose and fell heavily, and his face was a depiction of pure hatred and loathing. A final gust of fire flared, but when it died the goblin was gone.

Cormell's shoulder numbed, and his breathing became labored. He slid to the ground, his energy spent. He didn't bother to touch the knife that protruded from his shoulder, feeling the poison from his abdomen already spreading rapidly. He knew that if the creature were to attack them now, there was little they could do. As the moments passed without incident, he suspected that the goblin had fled, due to his injury. Or, Cormell thought, *he knows his poison will finish things.*

He heard Aden nearby but hadn't the strength to answer. He gazed up at the sky, watching as the tiny lights emerged slowly from the darkness. The day was over; the dwindling light on the horizon was the only sign of what had preceded the night. Cormell had envisioned a different ending to this day, regretting that he wouldn't get to return to the citadel with his trainee and celebrate another successful mission.

But Aden was safe.

The boy would live on, growing stronger with the passing of each day. Cormell silently chided himself one last time. Not a boy, but a young man. In his last moments, he took comfort in knowing Aden would survive this, that the creature hadn't truly won. He smiled inwardly as the poison reached his heart.

Aden is....

1

KNIGHTS FALL

"You are not ready to walk alone."

The same dream plagued him, as it had every night since that day. He saw Guardian Cormell in the distance, talking to someone obscured by the blazing cart. Aden was too far away to hear the conversation, but he recognized the tension in Cormell's demeanor. He tried calling through the verge stone again, but he received no answer.

Aden crept toward the stranger from behind, intending to give his mentor a tactical advantage if a fight ensued. He heard Cormell's warning, but had already activated the rune at his feet. Before he was able to react, the magic surrounded him and held him in place. Every failed effort to escape the restraining forces only succeeded in fueling his frustrations. Some movement at the edge of his vision caught his attention and two eel-like creatures slithered through the air around him. He could only watch as their sharp teeth sank deep into his flesh. He withstood the agony, but what came next made him cry out. A strand of electricity zapped him from the static charge that had grown thick in the air. An intense searing pain stung him and spread through his body like liquid fire. He called out to Cormell, even as the eel creatures drained his energy, wishing he was fighting beside his guardian where he belonged. Instead, he had to endure the torments of his prison while Cormell battled on.

His heart pounded harder with each bolt of current that struck him. A final shock burned through him as the debilitating magic vanished. He collapsed to the ground and closed his eyes as his head swam with dizziness. His aching body begged for rest, but he forced himself to stand. He moved sluggishly toward Cormell, with only his will to fuel him.

He attempted to run, but his body felt heavy, making his movements slower and the distance seem longer. Unlike the first time he'd witnessed Cormell fall, he knew the horrific outcome. The pain took hold. Sweat slid down his skin and panic seized him. He fell, but refused to give in and crawled forward. He was desperate to make it this time, but was forced to relive it again. The goblin escaped Cormell's magic and moved in close to his victim, and when the creature stepped back, Aden saw the bloodied knife.

No! his mind roared.

Aden fought to rise to his feet, but his body wouldn't obey. He was helpless as the goblin cast his magic and watched Cormell's effort to stop it. Tears stung Aden's eyes, and his heart ached. Nothing could change what had happened. Nothing.

He wanted to call a warning, but the dream wouldn't let him. Something flashed as Cormell succeeded in breaking the inferno. The dream then allowed him to be by Cormell's side. Aden trembled; it was already too late. His mentor was gone, his eyes now vacant of life.

Outraged, he looked around frantically for the murderer, but found only shadows.

The dream usually ended there, either to wake him with tears or leave him in the black bliss of sleep. This time, however, he was suddenly thrust into something new.

Fear gripped him here as well, but in a different way. He felt hunted, and so very alone. He struggled for breath, and every muscle was past the point of exhaustion. Why was he tired? He was always so tired. In desperation he used his power to help enhance his muscles and steady his movements. Even now, as he gasped for air, he used his abilities to remain standing. Darkness edged into his vision. He shook his head to ward off the fatigue. He would fight to his last breath.

He was cornered. He sensed the blades surrounding him, unsheathed with the promise of death. The wielders were mere shadows, faces hidden in the dim light. He heard their laughter as they advanced toward him. One shadow was more prominent than the rest, lighter than the others, its face barely visible. The figure took a step forward.

Aden raised his sword before him. "S-stay back!" he tried to shout boldly, but instead sounded as desperate as he felt.

The figure reached out with its free hand, but whether

pointing or beckoning, Aden was unsure. He felt drawn somehow, and something compelled him to lower his weapon. Then a voice whispered and echoed through the air.

"*Aden...*"

On a nearby table, the smooth-polished rock lit up and pinged another tone. Aden jolted from his sleep and shakily got to his feet. He touched the aphix stone and used it to connect with the mind of another.

"*Aden Fendrie, the keepers are ready to see you, and request your presence in the meeting hall.*"

He took a deep breath and responded with his own thoughts, before cutting the connection. "*On my way.*"

The keepers. A name given to those whose duty was to manage the citadel they were assigned. It was common that three keepers made up what was called the Council at each fortress. The office was given to distinct members of the Avant Guard, appointed by the magisters, the leaders and highest Council of the Order. A position of superior status, there was no higher rank, a station he'd never be worthy of. He did hope to one day become a guardian, as Cormell had been. It was an honorary title, bestowed to knights who had achieved a remarkable feat or displayed exemplary skill.

As he wiped perspiration from his forehead, Aden's eyes wandered to his sword propped against his bed. Knights of the Avant Guard, or the Ordained as some called them, never willingly parted with their weapons. As a knight in training, better known as a kit, he too revered his blade. He gripped the hilt and lifted the sword, the lack of weight a wonder to him ever since it was made. With the weapon sheathed at his hip, he headed for the meeting hall.

He had traveled the sunlit corridors countless times before, and his feet carried him through the routine. Distracted by his thoughts, he mindlessly returned the gesture when people waved in greeting. It had been fifteen days since the death of his guardian. He should be out there assisting with the investigation, but the keepers had ordered him to remain at the citadel. At first, they reasoned that his physical recovery from the ordeal was imperative, but the healer's magic had been thorough, and he'd quickly regained his strength. Now he was to simply wait while *they* looked into it. He was never good at waiting, especially when his guardian was the one who'd been murdered. He wanted answers!

Perhaps they uncovered a lead, or maybe decided he was able to join the search. Since Cormell's death, Aden was no longer content with being a mere trainee. His fierce ambition to advance to knighthood was driven by his desire to find his mentor's killer. Cormell's sword hadn't been found, either, and Aden felt sick as he imagined the murderer flaunting it as a trophy. He was determined to get it back and return it to the fires in which it had been forged, as was their custom.

He had presented a request for knighthood to the keepers, but he still awaited their final decision. Now he wavered somewhere between kit and knight, the Council refusing to give him an answer until the loss of Cormell was resolved. He understood their decision, but that knowledge did nothing to quell his frustrations. He needed his knight status to investigate for himself.

To keep his mind busy, he'd helped to train younger members in the use of weapons. It wasn't long before the instructors insisted they could handle the kits themselves, and all he was left with was more waiting.

He arrived at the meeting room door, and all further thoughts vanished as the attendant ushered him in. The room had always held a serene atmosphere, magnified by the breathtaking view through the windows. On one side, the ocean seemed to go on forever as it stretched beyond the horizon, while boats dotted its expanse as they sailed the treacherous waters. Contrasting this, a wondrous scene of building tops revealed the city's presence, while beyond its borders the mixed greens of the forest hid their own danger and mystery. Sunlight streamed through a corner of the window and warmed the feet of one of the several decorative white statues —heroic knights of old whose likeness had been captured in that moment. The stone figures stood against the walls while the three keepers sat in chairs, each in their own corner of the room.

Aden took his place in the center of it all. He waited silently, forcing his body to remain still, knowing the keepers would be observing him closely.

"Trainee Fendrie, we have reached a decision." Keeper Representative Harro Kalpus, whose long gray hair was tied back and away from his wrinkled face, spoke for the Council. "We've decided to deny your request for knighthood." The man held up a hand to forestall any forthcoming protest from

Aden, and he continued. "For the time being." He indicated the woman next to him. "We have asked for Guardian Ohn'na Sazi to take you on as her student."

Guardian Sazi stood with a warm smile. She was shorter than an average human woman, which suggested a dwarf lineage. Dwarves were few in the Avant Guard, but a mix-blood was rarer still. Human and elf members held the majority number in the Order.

Aden took a few breaths before he spoke, processing what the keeper had said. "With all due respect, Guardian Cormell was murdered, and I will not rest until I find his killer. I am ready for this task." He caught Guardian Ohn'na Sazi and Keeper Nannelle exchanging glances. Aera Nannelle was a dwarf member of the Council, and the one to his right.

Representative Kalpus shook his head. "That's what troubles us. You do not realize the effect your guardian's death is having on you. You are still struggling with it."

Aden bowed his head, keeping his voice low when he felt like shouting instead. "Cormell was more than my mentor, he was my friend. Of course I feel something. There's a part of me that wishes to find the one who did it and..." He couldn't complete the thought, shame making him falter. "But truly, I wish only to uncover why this happened and find justice."

"Since you speak honestly, we will tell you what we've learned of Guardian Cormell's death." Kalpus skimmed the room to ensure there were no objections, then continued. "We believe you were lured into a mercenary's trap. If it hadn't been you and Cormell, it would have been others. In the past few years, there have been increased aggressions against our

Order. We are searching for the source of it, but in the meantime the attacks continue and knights are either assassinated or go missing."

For a moment Aden was speechless, then his anger boiled to the surface. "Why haven't you announced this to everyone? Maybe if we were warned—"

"All understand the risks of being Ordained, the danger is no greater than before. Members should always be cautious of attacks against them." The third keeper, Zarie Jormus spoke, an older woman with deep frown lines set into her face. "And the magisters don't want to add any more trouble to the situation. We will handle this quietly, which will allow the transition back to normal to go more smoothly."

Aden didn't agree, but Representative Kalpus interjected before he could argue.

"The mercenaries we've questioned have been very forward with the information we demand. They claim there is an anonymous bounty on the Order, and those who acquire the blemished weapons from slain knights will be well rewarded. All attempts to follow this lead have only resulted in failure. Somehow, they are being alerted to our traps. We arrest those in possession of our blades and anyone who tries to accomplish such hostilities. We still have no answers, but our search remains ongoing."

Kalpus clasped his hands behind his back and hesitated before he spoke again.

"As for the mercenary you encountered, we haven't been able to track him down. Goblins are masters at disappearing when they feel the need. I'm sorry... his trail has gone cold. He vanished after the attack." Sympathy was clearly etched on the keeper's face. It was obvious that the man hoped Aden might find it easier to put the past behind him with this information.

A bounty? Aden thought. *Anyone could have put a bounty on the Order. We have so many enemies.* To find the instigator behind it would be next to impossible, and if the trackers couldn't find the goblin, he had little chance to do better. He knew he shouldn't give up hope, but he felt it slip away, to be replaced by the deep ache of guilt.

I shouldn't have suggested we split up. It's all my fault.

Outwardly he remained still, unlike the feelings that raged within him. "Thank you for informing me."

"We'd like you to remain posted under Guardian Sazi, until that time when she determines you are ready for knighthood," Representative Kalpus continued. "She hasn't taken a kit before now, but we believe you will benefit from her guidance."

"But I—" Aden began, but was interrupted by an all too familiar voice.

"In times like these we struggle with ourselves, and that is when we are most vulnerable to the demose. You should embrace this opportunity. You are not ready to walk alone," Keeper Nannelle added.

Aden returned the stare from those wise eyes. *You are not ready to walk alone.* How many times had she said those words to him, or some variation, when he'd tried to sneak out of the citadel? Nannelle had always been there waiting, no matter how he tried. They would then walk and talk as if that's what they'd planned to do all along. Eventually, Aden would give up for the night and return to bed.

Finally, one night she hadn't been there, acknowledging his determination and the need to return to where Cormell had fallen. After hours of searching, Aden hadn't found any clues as to where the goblin had gone, and he'd vented his rage to the night air. When he'd returned to the citadel, distraught and miserable, Keeper Nannelle had been waiting for him. She hadn't scolded him for leaving, and had only listened while he shared his pain with her. Aden was grateful for the kindness and patience she'd shown him while he worked through his grief.

He sighed in resignation. "If that is your wish." At least he could finally leave this place.

"That is all." Kalpus dismissed him.

Aden bowed and left the room, conscious of Guardian Sazi's eyes upon him and the fact that she hadn't said a word throughout the entire meeting.

Guardian Ohn'na Sazi opened the freshly bound book and studied it carefully. Records were kept for all within the Order, and she now held one such document. It was a detailed account about Aden, but only a replica. The original text would remain in the records hall for safekeeping, but as requested, the scribes had prepared a copy for her. The writing shimmered slightly, revealing the magic that infused the pages.

It had been enchanted so it could mirror the primary manuscript, showing any newly added entries.

Ohn'na read a passage that began with an overview of information about the young man. Aden Fendrie. A human male with amber eyes, who has been with the Avant Guard since childhood. He became a kit in early boyhood, and excelled in the use of weapons and wyvernkin riding. His grasp of the arcane art was typical for someone of his age, and his control of willful magic was delayed but showed promise. When Ohn'na read the latest entry about his guardian's death, she sympathized with the trainee's situation wholeheartedly.

Ohn'na had known Guardian Brant Cormell through reputation alone, but the man's deeds confirmed those rumors. She regarded her predecessor with the utmost respect and recognized the difficulty of defeating such a dangerous enemy while protecting his pupil. She felt the responsibility of her new role weigh heavily on her shoulders. She didn't have the years of experience Cormell had, but she immediately dismissed any doubts that crept into her thoughts. The keepers wouldn't have chosen her for the assignment unless she could help Aden finish the last of his training.

She had been free and able to take on a student, but the keepers had asked her so abruptly that there was an undeniable urgency to the request. Now she understood why. The kits were in danger. The mercenaries were targeting them, to gain advantage in battle by exploiting their inexperience and raw abilities. This tricky tactic was costing lives and increasing the risk to both knight and novice. Training programs were being accelerated, but the threat would remain until the bounty on the Order was removed and those behind it were dealt with.

Until then, the Order would need to remain vigilant. The keepers had to be careful in the decisions they made, and as such, Ohn'na saw the wisdom in denying Aden his request. If he were to become a knight now, he would be a tempting mark despite his progress. As Keeper Nannelle had pointed out, he needed more time. Before he could move forward, he had to prove that he was able to resist the demose, and come to terms with his loss. It was evident from the meeting that Aden still cared about his mentor a great deal, making what he had to face no easier.

In the bricf time she'd observed the kit, a unique feeling of resolve filled her. She was meant to be here, and her instincts were rarely wrong. She had sensed the powers that were growing in him, and with such promise, his untapped potential could elevate him to become as strong as any keeper. With time, he may come to rival anyone, even...

She shook her head, refusing to think of her old friend. She sighed as the moments passed and her thoughts still lingered there. She closed the book in her palm and sauntered to her open window, leaning against the frame as she peered out. "Frafnar... what are you doing now, I wonder?" She watched the people walk by below, but her focus was distant, in another place and time.

2

———

DARK WHISPERS

"A demose as well?"

Aden succumbed to grief that night, letting the waves of emotion rack his body. Hours later, he fell into an exhausted sleep. He was spared the horrid visions of reliving Cormell's death, but neither did he sink into the bliss of deep sleep. As they had the night before, his dreams led him down a different path. Darkness surrounded him, but that did nothing to hinder his sense that he wasn't alone. The other presence seemed to notice him as well, and he felt as if he was being dissected.

"I know your pain." The voice was low, but rose above other unintelligible whispers. *"Join with me, and we can be rid of it."*

"I will never join with the likes of you!" Aden shouted in his mind. *"Begone, demon!"*

The demose answered before the kit forced it away. *"We shall see."*

In the time since his guardian's death, Aden had found himself a frequent target of the demose—demons who wished to gain a foothold in Mythreth by binding with willing hosts. They would prey on the desperate, the vengeful, or the greedy. Victims who relented to their enticing promises did so at great cost. It was believed that once corrupted, their humanity was lost. Now driven by a lust for power, they would revel in the misery and suffering of others.

Anyone who was able to use magic was in danger of being tempted by the demose, but they focused heavily on the Ordained. This was not only due to their ability to use all forms of magic, but their capacity to alter it as well. This unique talent to transmute magic was commonly named willful magic, or *gritt* by others. All members of the Avant Guard were able to wield this rare power, with varying degrees of skill. Magisters were masters of the art, followed by the prominent keepers. The Order would search for individuals with this power—which was regarded as superior to other magic—to help teach them to resist the temptations of the demose. Those who chose to join with demons became known as Remnents.

Aden relaxed, feeling more at ease now that the demon was gone. Something began to bother him, though, like an itch he couldn't pinpoint or a light obscured through the trees. The more he settled himself, the stronger the feeling grew. It started vague and distant, just out of reach, but gradually drew closer. He soon realized he was no longer alone.

"Who... are... you...?" an unfamiliar voice questioned while the presence inspected him. Each word was drawn out, as if it was speaking to an infant. The voice was thick with deception and arrogance, and suggested a sharp intelligence. It chilled Aden to the core.

"I could ask you the same thing," Aden dared to answer, but with a degree of caution.

"It's impressive how easily you dismissed the lower demose, but count yourself fortunate it wasn't me." The weight of the voice alone made Aden feel lucky indeed. This presence was a powerful demon, so why wasn't it trying to convince him to submit? He couldn't help but feel a shade insulted.

"I agree. He wouldn't last a heartbeat." This voice belonged to a new presence Aden had failed to notice, but he sensed it wasn't a demon.

"What is this? What's going on?"

The others ignored him, however, now focusing on each other.

"Another soul has connected with yours, and at such a distance. This is rare." The demose huffed. *"Have you done this? Are you trying to hide something? You cannot deceive me!"*

"If you can explain how I could have possibly done this, please do. You're the one with eons of knowledge."

The connection was slipping away, the voices becoming more distant. The demon snorted, ignoring him completely, and broke the link. The mortal, though, focused his attention back on Aden. The vaguely familiar voice sounded like a whisper now.

"Who are you?"

Somewhere far away from the citadel, silvery-gray eyes opened to the darkness of the room. He knew the mental bond was real, his mind and soul having touched another's without the aid of spells. It hadn't lasted long enough to discover its source, but he sensed it was uncorrupted. The encounter had drained much of his energy, even as he slept.

He sat up in bed, brushing the damp hair from his face, his hand shaking from the effort. If it were to happen again, he would have to ensure he was in a secure location. No need for an enemy to seize the opportunity while he was powerless. Even now he was on edge, despite being safe in his quarters. He felt the demose inside, pushing at the edges of his will and testing his resolve. He couldn't afford to lose his inner strength.

Enemies all around, and even within. He shook his head and slightly chuckled at the irony of it all. He sat thinking for some time until a low tone drew his attention. Nearby, the dull yellow light of the smooth aphix stone had changed to red, and the white spinning runes morphed to black. A meeting had been called.

Aden roamed the darkened corridors, unable to sleep. The

lamps cast their luminescence every few feet, showing the way. Orbs of magical light sat atop them, their sizes ranging from large to small. The magical spheres would spin around each other, the smaller orbiting the larger. They could be an array of colors as well, but the keepers preferred the orange, yellow, and white.

Aden stopped to watch, his mind resembling the light— inescapable and going in circles. After a time, he pressed on and headed toward the upper stables. Unlike the lower stables, these sheltered large wyvernkin. The creatures weren't of this world, having to be summoned from another. They were a species similar to the rare dragons known to mortals, but usually smaller and simpleminded. The Avant Guard used their powers to tame and ride the creatures, but ordinary mages were never successful. The wyvernkin could only stay in Mythreth for an allotted period of time before their energy would drain away, and they'd fade back to their home.

Aden walked to the large summoning circle. He waved his hands, using his powers to light the candles surrounding it and infuse the runes with magic, making them glow. The creature slowly merged with this world, beginning as transparent and becoming more solid until it stood before him. The wyvernkin eyed Aden, uneasy at first, until he touched the creature's mind with his own. It let him approach and stroke its neck.

"He's a beauty."

The voice startled Aden and made him look over his shoulder. The wyvernkin remained still and composed. "Keeper Nannelle, you've found me again."

The old dwarf stepped closer, with her hands clasped

casually behind her back. "It *is* the last night I can talk you out of leaving."

For a moment there was silence, except for the night wind that blew around them. "I was actually hoping you would," he finally admitted, then told her about his dream and how he'd connected with another.

"Oh?" Keeper Nannelle raised an eyebrow. "A demose as well?"

"Yes," Aden replied, "but it appeared as though the demon hadn't completely merged with the person."

"Your connection was unusual indeed. There are many that accept the demose, and reasons for doing so are more numerous still. Narrowing down their identity might take some time. Until you learn more, there isn't much we can do."

Thinking of dealing with that demon again made Aden shiver. "Do you think this could be linked to Guardian Cormell?"

"His death has certainly made you more vulnerable. More than that, I cannot say."

Silence fell between them again, and the wyvernkin stretched its wings eagerly. Noticing this, the keeper gave him a small smile. "Let the night air clear your mind, Aden Fendrie. Just promise you'll come back."

Aden returned her smile with one of his own. "I promise."

3

—————

HOPE

"Nothing is certain."

The next morning, Aden was informed that Guardian Sazi wanted to meet him in the gardens. As he made his way through the corridors, something caught his attention at the edge of his vision, like a person standing against the wall watching him. However, when he looked there was nothing. Aden shook his head. This had been happening recently and far too often. Maybe he was losing it, still expecting his old guardian to show up and everything to be as it was. He continued down the hall.

When Aden arrived in the gardens, he found Ohn'na Sazi sitting and enjoying herself in the sun. Now, when not under the scrutinizing eyes of the keepers, Aden could fully comprehend his new mentor. She had her hair tied back, but the loose parts played in the breeze as the golden strands basked in the sunlight. There was a rumor that she was actually a druid—if not partly. If that was true, it was obvious that her druid blood largely overshadowed her dwarf heritage, her stature and slightly muscular frame notwithstanding. Druids physically appeared like humans, but never aged past thirty. Only her rank in the Order disclosed her years, since it was uncommon for junior knights to attain the title of guardian.

From this distance, Aden could still feel the power from the woman, and he caught himself comparing her to Cormell. The memories caused an emotional stir inside him. Unable to face it, he turned to collect his composure and collided with someone.

"Oh, I'm sor—" Aden began automatically. "Khodi?"

"I never expected a body slam. I guess it's what I get for trying to sneak up on you." The girl picked herself off the ground and patted her clothing.

"Sneak up on me?"

"Well, we were sparring partners after all. I just wanted to test if your reflexes are still as sharp as they used to be." Khodi noticed a leaf in her red hair and she plucked it off. "Plus, I had called to you, but you didn't hear me."

"I-I guess I was a little distracted," Aden replied.

Khodi's expression turned serious. "I'm sorry about Guardian Cormell." She reached out and gently hugged him. "You know, I'm here for you. I... oh, not now, you old bat!"

The trainee searched her pockets until she produced a

small, smooth rock. The verge stone pulsed with light and shook with its own vibrations. Some things never changed.

"Freesha still running you ragged, is she?" Aden asked, ready to change the subject.

Khodi looked at him mournfully. "All her years at the citadel have not diminished her by-the-book ways. I'm starting to think I'll never be a knight at this rate." Then there was a twinkle in her eye. "My theory is that she enjoys my suffering as her lackey, secretly plotting how to make me remain her trainee forever. Seriously, though, I don't know what the Council was thinking. She's getting too old; soon she'll have to enjoy the perks of retirement, or promotion as keeper. Divine take pity on her subordinates if that happens."

Aden rolled his eyes and grinned. It was good to see his friend again. It felt like old times.

"Good, a smile. You're lucky, I was this close to bringing out the yeti jokes." Khodi closed the distance between her thumb and index finger but then caught sight of who was in the garden. "Isn't that...?"

Aden nodded after following her gaze.

"Wow, Guardian Ohn'na Sazi," she continued, totally enthralled. "You know she hasn't taken any kits before? Word has been circulating that she was pressured to take one."

When Aden said nothing and only stared at her, Khodi's jaw dropped. "Not you! I was sure the Council would agree you are ready for knighthood."

"I guess not." He couldn't hide his disappointment.

Khodi grasped his shoulder lightly, with a reassuring smile.

"Don't worry about it, I'm sure... Can't a person comfort their friend for one minute!" she finished loudly as a small bird now hovered above her, poking her urgently on the head.

It was Freesha's own personal pet, which was often used to track down her kit if she was absent for an extended period and hadn't reported in.

"I have to go or Freesha's going to have a bird—oh wait, she already sent one!" Khodi waved off the bird like an annoying insect. "We only just returned and we're off on another mission, but we will definitely catch up soon."

Aden watched as his friend left, swatting at the bird that continued to pester her. He and Khodi had become trainees at around the same time, and had been friends ever since. It was almost fate, or deliberate planning, that they were chosen to spar together. They had complemented and improved each other's shortcomings well, with Khodi's proficiency in spells and Aden's natural talent with a blade.

He turned back to where Guardian Sazi was waiting and took a deep breath. If Khodi could face Freesha, Aden could face his own demons.

"Was I not clear? There are to be no more *accidents* within the ranks until our forces have reached a capacity to my satisfaction."

A ghostly dark-cloaked figure appeared before those in the room, the face concealed but the voice obviously feminine. A book of power lay open under the projected image of their leader, with the communication runes speeding across the pages as if in their own panic.

"Yes, Mistress," the captain began. "But—"

"It appears you are not as competent as I once believed," the image continued coolly, although each word was as sharp as steel.

"No, it was one of my men..." The panic in the man's voice was evident, along with a hint of anger.

Frafnar smirked from behind his mask. Framing his superior had almost been too easy.

A rune manifested beneath the nervous man, growing around him. He tried to run, but his feet were already ensnared by the magic. The rune's growth stopped and spun slowly, red and menacing.

"I grow tired of you and your excuses," the Mistress said.

When he attempted to release himself from her hold, she barely flinched and made a movement with her hand. The man's body burst into flames, and his screams filled the air. The others in the room dared not move; they simply watched as their captain died. The Mistress then turned to the masked man beside the smoldering corpse.

"Frafnar Armastus. You will replace him. Fail me as he did, and your death will not be as pleasant."

"As you wish, Mistress." Frafnar bowed.

The image flickered slightly, then disappeared completely.

The guards stationed around the room slipped back into the shadows. They were loyal agents and protectors of the

Mistress, who presided over the meetings. One lingered, however, catching Frafnar's attention. During his time with the renegades, he'd come across several goblins, but this one had no reservations about showing his true form. The creature noticed the man observing him, and tipped his hat in acknowledgment. Frafnar did his best to meet the goblin's gaze but couldn't ignore the ghostly hand that extended from the stub at his wrist, or the tarnished Avant Guard weapon on his belt. The sword was blatantly donned as a trophy, secured there for all to see. Frafnar was careful to smother his emotions, before they sabotaged his calm demeanor and exposed his true sentiments.

When the creature finally merged into the darkness, Frafnar breathed a little easier. He eyed the smoking husk of his predecessor. It was a testament to the consequences of failure, and its costly price. He would have to tread carefully, but the men he commanded were loyal, he'd made sure. Anyone who had shown signs of dispute or betrayal he'd disposed of. Frafnar was now closer to his goal, but what that was... he struggled with, at times. And now, when the timing was crucial, his attention was divided. No, he had to stay focused, or all this would be for nothing. He strode from the room, comfortably fitting into his new role, feeling it had been his all along.

Keeper Nannelle looked out to the horizon from one of the many windows in the meeting chamber. As hard and as often as she tried, she couldn't sense him anymore, but the connection in Aden's vision had given her hope. There were too many possibilities, but her mind kept churning over the one too difficult to entertain. It couldn't be him. He was too involved now to safely contact the Order. Perhaps it was a call for help. Either way, whether it was him or not, it didn't bode well.

Nannelle bent her head. She replayed the question raised by Keeper Kalpus during their meeting earlier that day.

"Do you think he's fallen?"

The words could have a double meaning, and she didn't want to consider either. Had he been killed, or had he embraced the demose? Given the situation, she had replied with the only answer she saw fit. She whispered the words again, refusing to give up hope.

"Nothing is certain."

As Aden approached, Guardian Ohn'na Sazi greeted him with a smile. "Friend of yours?"

It appeared she had spotted his run-in with Khodi. "Ah, yeah. She was just leaving on another mission. Sorry I'm late, Guardian Sazi."

Ohn'na motioned toward the seat next to her. "Please, come sit." Once he'd done so, she continued. "Firstly, I'd prefer if you'd call me Ohn'na. There's no need for formalities. I am your ally, and we will need to work closely together to overcome the trials ahead."

Aden's hopes rose, and he dared ask, "So, you will support my request to become a knight?"

Ohn'na placed her hand on his. "Once I see for myself how far you've progressed, perhaps then." When his shoulders slumped in disappointment, she gave him a reassuring pat. "If there's anything you'd like to know, don't hesitate to ask. Since we are working together, we should be comfortable doing so. I understand that you considered Cormell a friend, and I hope that you'll come to view me as such as well."

Despite his somber mood, Aden was surprised it had turned out like this. He never expected Ohn'na to be this way, so open and friendly. She was, after all, a respected guardian. Aden was sure Khodi would proclaim her jealousy, as she had with Cormell.

"Well," Aden began, choosing his words carefully, "there was one thing that had crossed my mind."

"Yes?"

As her deep blue eyes stared into his, Aden sensed a keen intelligence behind them, as well as wisdom beyond her years. He almost stopped himself, but his curiosity forced the words from him.

"Why haven't you taken a kit before now?"

"Ah, a query I'm sure many young members have been wondering about." She sighed. "But a fair one."

Ohn'na folded her arms as if collecting her thoughts, perhaps searching where to begin. Just when Aden thought she had changed her mind, she spoke.

"I suppose I never felt quite ready, maybe even unfit, despite the keepers' blessings. They never assigned a trainee to me, until now. You see, I too lost my mentor, so I can relate to your feelings."

"I'm sorry." Aden truly meant it. He'd recently endured the pain of such loss, and he recognized that in Ohn'na's expression. "Do... you mind if I asked what happened?"

She met his eyes squarely. "I killed him."

4

GUILT

"Forgive yourself."

I *killed him.* Ohn'na offered this blunt truth, with no rush to explain. She hesitated, as if surrendering to any judgment that came her way. Aden was speechless, and more than relieved when she began.

"I remember his son, Garret. He'd become a strong knight, like his father. They had him stationed at a distant outpost on the outskirts of tamed land, but he would visit the citadel from time to time when missions brought him to the area. Then *that* incident happened, a few years after Frafnar joined with us."

"Frafnar?"

"Ah yes, you wouldn't know of him, even though he'd be around your age now, if not a little older. He was a trainee with great potential, apparently able to do anything despite his heritage. I even envied him. He was only twelve seasons old when he joined with Knight Servol Raismus and me. Usually the keepers forbid anyone to take on more than one trainee, but in Frafnar's case they made an exception. No other knights were willing to take a mix-blood orc into their care, but Raismus welcomed the challenge with enthusiasm." Ohn'na stared into the distance. "It was a great honor, but Raismus never got the chance to tell Garret the news."

She paused for a moment, as though deep in thought, then continued. "It's unfortunate that not all who seek to become members of the Order are accepted. Only the best are chosen. It has always been this way. Some leave on their own for various reasons, and the others who are not selected to train with a knight are dismissed. In peacetime, we can have an overabundance of members and a lack of available posts. I'm certain this was the reason the Council hadn't assigned a trainee to me."

The guardian sighed. "There are some who become bitter and resentful for being discharged, despite the normal lives they can lead. They have a unique advantage with their abilities and fundamental training, but I guess some don't have the knack for adjustment as others do. The group that captured Garret definitely fell under the less gifted category. They demanded a ransom from the Order in exchange for his life. The keepers were also warned that if there was any rescue attempt, they would kill their hostage without hesitation. Despite this, Raismus pleaded with the Council to help his son, confident the Order could save him. He was certain the renegades would kill Garret either way. The keepers disagreed and continued their negotiation attempts. Raismus disobeyed the Order. When he got there, his fears had been confirmed and all he found of his son was bone and ash."

Her voice became soft and quiet. "I remember his eyes, when he returned alone. They were cold, distant. He blamed the keepers for his son's death and left the Order, tracking down the group himself. At what point he decided to join with the demose, I do not know." Ohn'na tugged on a strand of stray hair. "I advanced to knighthood before Raismus left, the keepers were confident I was ready. Frafnar had also requested knighthood, knowing how difficult it had been to find a mentor the first time. The Council denied him, however, and he left with Raismus."

Aden could relate to that: feeling ready for promotion while others believed otherwise. He didn't know Frafnar but empathized with him. He couldn't imagine leaving the Order, though.

"Soon after," Ohn'na continued, "we learned that Raismus was planning to attack the Council directly during one of their meetings, using other rejected recruits known as renegades. Thankfully, our group found them before they carried out their plan. I tried to convince the renegades to turn away from the demose, but they wouldn't listen. Frafnar disappeared after Raismus fell, and I often wonder what happened to him. Goes to show how even the most dedicated of us can be swayed by the demons."

"It's almost like we can't care about anything or anyone at all, or the demose use it against us," Aden whispered.

"No." Ohn'na shook her head. "That's what separates us

from the Remnents. We can feel joy, grief, regret, pain, love. These remind us of our purpose, to protect those we care about. Joining with the demons is a lonely road, full of selfishness, anger, fear, and hate. It takes a strong will to be Ordained."

Aden nodded slowly and mulled it over. They sat in a part of the garden that saw few visitors, and he was glad for the privacy so he could absorb the information without interruption.

After a time, she took a deep breath before she began. "Now Aden, what are your *true* feelings? When you were before the keepers, I sensed an inner conflict beyond your words." When Aden said nothing, she tried again. "Have you seen or heard Guardian Cormell of late?"

It dawned on Aden what Ohn'na was hinting at, and he stared at her. Of course, they could communicate with the recently fallen, especially someone close to them and whose spirit hadn't left this world yet. After a time, if the spirit refused or was unable to move on, the memories of their lives would fade. They would then become nothing but vessels of hate and resentment for the living. He had no prior experience with such things and had been so consumed with his inner turmoil he'd forgotten.

"I... no."

"Your suffering is closing off the connection," Ohn'na explained. "Perhaps your spirit can be opened enough to reforge that bond. We can try now, if you wish."

Aden was a little reluctant but felt compelled to try. He sat cross-legged on the grass in the shade of the trees and closed his eyes, exhaling to still his reeling thoughts. He reached out with his mind, as he'd been taught. Truthfully, he felt responsible for Cormell's death and wasn't eager to face him.

"Now just remember one thing." Ohn'na spoke as if she'd read his mind. "His death wasn't your fault. Some things are out of our control."

"You know, she's absolutely right."

Aden's eyes snapped open at the sound of the familiar voice. In that moment, the breeze swayed the tree branches enough that the sun found holes in the shade and blinded him. When the instant passed he saw the ghostly echo of Cormell leaning against a tree. His old friend seemed like an ordinary man, but his range of skills set him apart from most. His kindness and humor were always verified by his words, even now, with his attention on Ohn'na.

"I like this girl, Aden. She has a good head on her shoulders. Pretty too."

"Why, thank you." Ohn'na blushed slightly. "Though no one has called me a girl for some time."

Startled, Cormell pointed an accusing finger at her. "You can see me?"

"Of course."

"And you never said anything?"

Ohn'na unveiled a guilty little smile. "Well, I assumed it was the trainee you sought."

"Cormell?" His quiet tone made them both shift their attention to Aden. "I'm sorry."

"What are you apologizing for?" Cormell crossed his arms. "Unless you mean for failing to see me."

Aden stood as a sudden rush of energy filled him. "That was you? I thought I was going crazy!"

"Perhaps if you'd noticed me, then you wouldn't have thought that!" Cormell stepped closer.

"You obviously had a very lively time together," Ohn'na said with an amused ring in her voice.

"I'm sorry," Aden repeated again, his energetic mood instantly dampened. "I shouldn't have suggested we split up. It... it was all my fault."

Cormell looked Aden straight in the eye. "No, Ohn'na is right. There was nothing you could have done. It was my time."

When Aden lowered his head and shook it in denial, the spirit refused to give up. "Aden, you did all you could. You withstood the goblin's magic, and that alone is no small feat." Cormell's voice softened. "I understand your pain, but revenge isn't our way. Don't fall to the darkness and let it win. Don't let my sacrifice be for nothing."

Aden stopped cold.

"Know that I found peace, and now find yours. You needn't mourn for me." He smiled at Aden. "We had some wild adventures, didn't we? Remember those times, I will always be there." Cormell held Aden's gaze with his own. "Now Ohn'na will be your guide. But would you fulfill one last duty for me?"

Aden straightened in readiness. "Anything."

"Forgive yourself."

Despite his surprise at such an unexpected request, Aden nodded to declare his willingness to try. Satisfied, Cormell started to walk down the path, but stopped beside Ohn'na. "Take care of him... for me." Then he whispered, "He can be a handful sometimes."

"I heard that!"

Both guardians laughed. Ohn'na affirmed her promise with a bow, and then Cormell continued on his way. Before his form faded, he held up a hand and waved without looking back. Then he was gone.

"Curse you, Zeffron!"

Frafnar's cool demeanor gave way to his rage. Zeffron's evil laughter filled his mind from the verge stone in his hand. He was tempted to throw it, but its usefulness stopped him.

"Well, well. It was a trap set for the previous captain, but seems I caught something more interesting."

"You better hope I die, because there will be no second chances."

"Oh, I'm certain you will. Reports of this land seem promising, even for someone like you. If you survive the fall, that is. Die well, Captain Armastus."

The connection was lost and Frafnar pounded a fist against the back of his mount, making it screech. He calmed himself and used his mind to do the same to the creature beneath him, which tilted its head in confusion. The corves resembled a giant crow, but with deep red eyes. They were much like the wyvernkin of the Order, as they too were summoned, albeit from the dark realms of the demose. Frafnar knew their masters never showed remorse for their actions, and he couldn't help but pity the beast.

There was nothing he could do. Zeffron had summoned the corves long before Frafnar left the fortress. Now the creature's energy was already spent, and soon it would fade back to its home. Frafnar stroked the feathered neck and felt the struggle put into each wingbeat.

He looked down to judge the distance to the ground. He probably could make it. With some luck, he hoped to land in one of the snaking rivers below. He didn't want to think about the alternative.

"Go home," Frafnar ordered. When the corves hesitated, he once again joined with the confused mind. *"Go home,"* he commanded more forcefully, and as the corves began to fade, he fell.

He cursed his luck. He knew Zeffron's motives were purely greed—another captain's thirst for control of more troops. It wasn't anything personal, but a threat Frafnar couldn't overlook. If he made it out of this, he'd be sure to kill the man.

Frafnar closed his eyes and stilled his mind to concentrate on survival. Just before the corves had completely gone, he sensed something from the creature he hadn't before. Gratitude. Despite the danger, he couldn't stop the small smile that slid across his face.

5

DETOUR

"The keepers are going to kill me."

Aden stood in his room once again while Ohn'na resolved a local dispute in the city before they left for their first mission. He had assured the guardian that he was able to accompany her on this small matter, but Ohn'na had insisted he take the few hours for himself. In truth, Aden was grateful. He had a lot to think about with the events that had taken place that morning. Seeing Cormell was an astonishing gift, and he felt like a great weight had been lifted from his shoulders. He hadn't forgotten his vow, however; he would find the goblin and retrieve Cormell's lost sword. The creature was still out there somewhere, but Aden had to focus on his duties until the mercenary was found.

For now, he was to meet Ohn'na in the citadel's upper

stables. Aden secured his weapon to his belt and wore the Order's customary travel cloak. No other preparations were necessary since the emergency supplies were packed and waiting for them. A strong feeling of sentiment washed over him as he scanned his quarters. At the head of his bed, sunlight filtered in through the window and chased away the shadows. In a corner of the room was a table with a lamp, the aphix stone, and some parchment paper. Aden could almost see a younger version of himself seated in the chair, bent over and snoozing soundly, exhausted from his studies. Paintings covered the walls, and he lingered on his favorite, a sleek wyvernkin. The room wasn't much, but it was home. A feeling crept in that this would be the last time here. The last time he would look out his window at the magnificent city he called home. Blaming it on anxiety, he shrugged off the sensation. Aden blinked and the feeling was gone. He took one last look around, at what would surely be waiting for him, then left.

The walk to the stables wouldn't take long. This citadel was nowhere near the size of the founding structures but was no less impressive. It sat atop a rocky cliff, climbing high into the sky like a lance protecting those below. It was appropriately named Longshield Citadel. Water from a large river flowed around it and tumbled into the ocean. The rest of Avender city was built around this, encompassing the citadel that stood as the highest building. It was believed that it had been established there so people knew where to go for guidance and were comforted by the protection. Unfortunately, some viewed it as a display of the Order's arrogance.

The beauty of the surrounding structures went unnoticed

as Aden made his way to the upper stables, his excitement increasing his pace with every step. He'd been grounded for too long. His short excursion the previous night did nothing to satisfy his desire for freedom. However, when he caught sight of the creature, all his restlessness fell away and was replaced by giddy joy. The majestic wyvernkin bathed in the light of the midmorning sun, embellishing the array of fiery reds and oranges in its scales. Much like a cat, the beast opened its maw in a great toothy yawn and stretched in a bow before curling up to snooze. Within moments, the creature was snoring lightly while waiting for its passengers. It was large enough to carry two, and Aden couldn't help but hope he would be permitted to navigate their journey.

Aden remained fixated on the wyvernkin as he considered the details of their assignment. They were to escort a supply caravan to a recently constructed outpost. If some considered Longshield a backwater settlement, this new citadel was in the middle of nowhere.

Aden was still admiring the wyvernkin when Ohn'na finally arrived.

"O-o-oh, I should never have eaten that—" She held a hand to her mouth, intent to keep down what was forthcoming.

Aden suspected more than words would have come out if she hadn't stopped herself, and was convinced he saw her actually change several shades of green in moments.

"I swear, those fiends use fighting as an excuse to try to sell their food to the Order, or enjoy watching us eat something like... like..." She failed to find the words, and her queasiness seemed to intensify.

Aden soon learned that one of the many tavern disputes had easily been solved, but Ohn'na had been coaxed into trying some of their new dishes. She'd been unable to deny the request without offending the owner, but her stomach wasn't accustomed to sampling such outrageous recipes.

"I got cornered, and either way I was done for," Ohn'na said while holding her stomach. "Listen, we need to get moving. Do you think you can handle flying while I recoup?"

Aden grinned wider than he meant to. His worry that she would call off the mission vanished instantly. "Of course! I've done this many times."

"Good." Ohn'na staggered to their mount, waving off any offer of help. As soon as she was secured in place, she was out cold.

Aden scratched his head, unsure what to make of the situation. From the fermented smell, it appeared that the tavern owners had given Ohn'na more than water to drink as well. He turned his head, seeing the empty rider's seat, then back at his guardian to check if she was truly asleep. When he was satisfied, he sprinted to the creature and jumped on. The wyvernkin, now awake and eager to fly, didn't hesitate to take to the air. Aden grinned wickedly. Since the rendezvous point wasn't far, he had time for the scenic route.

He guided the wyvernkin high above the city, heading for the ocean. When he reached the cliff he made a steep dive then pulled up when they were close to the shore. He skimmed the surface of the water, dodged a couple boats, then veered back to land. Outside the city a great expanse of forest still thrived, the trees huge and ancient. Aden steered between the great trunks, having more than enough room to maneuver. With time running short, he finally veered back to the city, his heart pounding and a delighted grin plastered across his face. He met the caravan at the designated location, along with the other knight escorts. Aside from remaining vigilant for plundering highwaymen, Aden and the knights could sit back and relax for most of the journey.

Hidden on a huge tree limb, Frafnar surveyed the creatures as they chased the illusion of himself. It wouldn't take long for them to catch up and discover that it was a trick, but it would give him enough time to contact his men. He used the verge stone to reach out with his mind, but he was still too far from them. To avoid any unnecessary casualties, he'd intended to scout the land before deploying his troops to search it. Fatalities would be difficult to explain to the Mistress and make him the new focus of her wrath. And so, he'd come alone, but he now cursed himself for such foolishness. The Mistress had prohibited captains from attacking each other, but by now he should have learned to expect anything. He grudgingly admitted that Zeffron's plan was creative, and a ploy he wished *he* had schemed up.

Frafnar was about to withdraw his consciousness when his senses detected someone familiar. He recognized the connection as the same mind that had visited his subconscious. This undisclosed person was much closer now, and he was desperate. Taking the chance given to him, Frafnar concentrated hard and put all his urgency behind the words. *"Find me!"*

"Here he is," a voice shouted nearby.

In one swift motion, Frafnar used a vine to swing from the limb and ran when his feet found solid ground. He hoped his message got through. If not, he'd only succeeded to give away his position to the creatures who hunted him.

Aden was restricted to maintain formation with the group and their straightforward flying. He longed to scout ahead and enact some maneuvers that would get his blood pumping, but unfortunately those positions had already been assigned to others while he had taken his sightseeing detour. There really wasn't anything else to do, but thankfully the citadel wasn't far now.

Ohn'na still rested soundly, and the trip was simply routine. Now, Aden almost wished for a highwayman attack or a windstorm. He'd even take a wyvernkin stomachache. But all was quiet, including the chatter between the travelers.

A strange feeling overcame him, similar to a hard pinch. He sensed the rough urgency from the other consciousness, and felt drawn to it, even though the source was obscure. It was somehow familiar. No one else seemed alerted to anything unusual, but for all he knew it could be an ally in trouble. He considered his options carefully. They were now close enough to the citadel that he was certain the others could finish escorting the caravan safely. Making up his mind, Aden informed the group of his departure. None argued with him, probably thinking it was Ohn'na's decision, and fixed their formation once Aden had left the lines. He considered apprising the guardian of the deviation, but decided to wait until he had more to report. She needed her rest, and there was no point in waking her with such little information at hand. Aden let his instincts guide him toward the source that called to him, but was unsure how long the journey would be. So far, the trip hadn't been strenuous on their wyvernkin. He was confident it could still last most of the day, but he presumed it wouldn't take that long.

To Aden's relief, the sun was just past high time when he felt they were close. He didn't detect anything unusual about the area. A sea of flora covered the terrain, and plenty of lakes and rivers snaked through the land. He couldn't sense the other presence anymore, but his gut told him this was the right place. He reached out with his mind, but there was no reply. Guiding the wyvernkin to fly lower until they were slightly above the treetops, he searched for any sign as to who'd called to him.

A sudden burst of light triggered Aden to bank the wyvernkin sharply to the side. His reflexes saved them as a stream of powerful magic passed along their flight path. He didn't know what would happen if it struck them, but he didn't want to find out. He felt the chill of panic when it turned and headed straight for them again. Dodging trees was nothing compared to the maneuvers demanded of him now. Whenever he tried to ascend, it would force him back down near the surface. What was going on?

The wyvernkin was an agile flying creature, and it responded instantly to his commands. If both rider and beast couldn't synchronize in battle, they were likely to perish. Aden was fortunate to have a natural talent for riding, which was essential now as the energy chased them. He had little time to think once the light streams split into six, each moving separately but visibly working together. Sweat beaded Aden's forehead and his heart raced as he concentrated, led only by his instincts. They were in trouble.

One of the magic rays clipped the wyvernkin, which threw them into a spin. Aden was flung from his seat and his body connected with a tree, plunging him into a deep darkness.

Ohn'na slowly recovered consciousness. Still groggy, she opened her eyes. She saw a tree limb sticking above her head, but it didn't register and she only patted the thing. "Good tree."

She stumbled on the large uneven branch. She had thought the nausea and lightheadedness would have worn off by now, but she wasn't so fortunate. Her head seemed to hurt even more. She saw Aden sitting on another branch nearby. "Where are we?"

"Um..." Aden's eyes moved side to side while he fiddled with his fingers. "We took a bit of a detour."

"A detour?" Ohn'na asked, but still rather dazed fell

through a gap in the rugged branches. A twisted maze of vines ensnared her feet and stopped her fall. She hung upside down with her arms crossed as she absorbed their situation. Indeed, they had not arrived at the citadel. An unfortunate outcome for her first mission with her first trainee. "The keepers are going to kill me."

"We are not Remnents!"

"This didn't go as well as I'd hoped," Aden said as he lowered the rest of their supplies to the ground.

"You did the right thing." Ohn'na sat nearby and was using restoration magic to heal her minor injuries and eliminate the rest of the nausea. "I don't know how many times I was pulled into one adventure or another."

"When we get back, you'll have to tell me all about it."

If they got back. The threat was still out there, and Aden could find no sign of who had drawn him here. Maybe it was a trap. Or the person was dead. Either way, their situation didn't look promising.

The wyvernkin was gone. It had returned to its home due to its injuries, but Aden was comforted by the knowledge that the creature couldn't be killed in this realm. With the beast's disappearance, their supplies were scattered throughout the area and Ohn'na and Aden were left with the chore to collect them. They were almost finished the work when the guardian noticed his head was damp on one side. Aden imagined that the blood blended well with his dark hair, but the experienced knight didn't miss it.

"Are you all right?"

He ran his fingers through the slick strands. "Yeah, I've already stopped the bleeding."

Ohn'na nodded; then she looked past him. "We have company."

Aden turned and saw a dark-cloaked figure standing nearby, a mask covering its face. He kept a hand close to his weapon, not solely due to the figure's appearance, but also the haunting silence of the approach.

"If you value your lives, you will follow me. Now." The voice was low and unnatural, which magnified its intimidating presence.

The mask had distinctive red markings that looked remarkably like eyes, which sent a chill through Aden. Dread lurked at the edge of his mind, but subsided when the figure sprinted past them.

Aden exchanged quick looks with Ohn'na, but sensed that indeed the stranger was telling the truth and something else was coming. They grabbed their packs of supplies and followed the newcomer. As soon as they were hidden by the trees and brush, Aden heard the growls behind them. The stranger's pace was fast and brutal, and yet he made little sound. Aden and Ohn'na easily matched his speed and silent movement, but they had training. Who was this guy? And what were they running from?

They had covered some distance when the masked man held up a gloved hand and indicated they should all get low. It was hard to see through the foliage, but Aden caught glimpses of the creatures ahead. They grunted an unfamiliar language as they made their way past them.

Several moments after the group had gone, Aden watched the stranger remove the mask, and Ohn'na's jaw dropped.

"Frafnar," she blurted, with a glint in her eyes. "It can't be."

Frafnar? Aden thought. It couldn't be the Frafnar who had traveled with Ohn'na and her mentor. The same man who had left the Order? That Frafnar? What was he doing all the way out here, of all places?

"You never did miss a thing, Ohn'na." Frafnar said and pulled back his hood.

Aden couldn't help but stare. Short black hair blew in the wind, making the silvery-gray eyes stand out even more. His skin was a dark bluish gray, and when he spoke the slightly larger canine teeth were visible. Ohn'na had explained that her old colleague had an orc father and a human mother, but the man's appearance still left him in a state of mild shock. These thoughts flew from Aden's mind, however, when those cold and calculating eyes focused on him. He didn't realize he'd been holding his breath until the half-orc reverted his attention to the guardian.

"It will be dark soon. I know a protected place where they

wouldn't dare go. We should rest there for the night and plan our next move."

Ohn'na nodded in agreement, but Aden wasn't so sure. It was plain that they had few options, but now there were more questions than answers. As they traveled, Aden remained with Ohn'na to safeguard the rear. After some time passed, he shared his concerns. He kept his voice low and his eyes glued on Frafnar's back as he spoke.

"Are you sure we can trust him? From the story you told me..."

Ohn'na shrugged. "If he was in league with the creatures, he wouldn't have aided us back there. Frafnar seems to know a little about them, so for the time being we should follow his lead. In any case, keep an eye out until we know more."

Once they arrived in an area the half-orc had deemed safe, Aden collected wood while Ohn'na made a fire pit and sparked the flames. The hour was rapidly growing late, and all worked quickly to finish their tasks before they lost the light. Frafnar had assured them that the creatures wouldn't attack, even if they gave away their position from the smoke. Aden was unloading another armful of branches when the half-orc returned with some dead animal in hand. It wasn't long before the meat was cooking above bright flames. While they waited, Ohn'na tossed a food pouch to each of them and kept one for herself. Then the trio sat and ate quietly, each deep in their own thoughts.

I remember how I hated these things, Frafnar thought as he eyed the food and took bites of it. *Like eating nutritious dry bread.* He waited in anticipation for the meat and split it between the three of them when it was ready. They couldn't afford to lose their energy to fight.

"Fraf, where have you been all this time?" Ohn'na broke the silence. "And why the mask? It makes you look... different."

He leveled a steely gaze toward her. "I think you should be more concerned with the draquor than about me."

Ohn'na paused for a moment. "What can you tell us about them?"

"I was stranded here, just like you are. From what I've learned of these draquor creatures, they have lived here for centuries. If living is what you could call it. Long ago, a Remnent used this area for experimentation, not unheard of in the wilds. At this particular site, he would kill and reanimate the draquor. He infused them with dark magic to turn them into a fierce army. These creatures were a primitive species, but their minds had potential to grow, and with that, their power. To his misfortune, the experiment was a failure in the end. The creatures became too difficult to control and they rebelled. The Remnent managed to escape, but the draquor continued to exist. They worship an artifact that gives them power and strength. I believe this is the key to putting them to rest, and also, perhaps we can find a means of escape as their master did."

Ohn'na rested an elbow on her raised knee. "There was a strange magic that attacked us. Do you know what it was?"

"There are elder draquor, stronger and wiser than the

rest, who can join their minds and manifest this power. They use it to ground any who pass into their territory. The draquor are excellent trackers and hunters. They can use and even sense magic, which makes them extremely dangerous. I would be gone from this place already if they could be taken down easily. Their sheer numbers make it even more difficult." Frafnar poked the fire with a stick to keep the flames alive. His clothes were torn in places, stained with blood and dirt. How many draquor had he fought already? He truly felt as ragged as he looked.

"How do you know all this?"

"Ah, I see your kit can speak, Ohn'na."

"My *name* is Aden, and I was to be a knight soon if—"

Frafnar smirked. "Is the Council still denying people... or just you?"

Aden straightened his posture. "At least I'm still with the Order."

Frafnar launched a disgusted look at the kit, then turned to Ohn'na. "I think someone's been talking about me."

Smiling sheepishly, Ohn'na shifted uneasily. "Well," she cleared her throat, "we never discussed why you left—"

"Isn't it obvious? I was angry at the keepers."

Ohn'na frowned. "I know you were on the brink of knighthood, but to follow Raismus was an impulsive decision. That's not like you."

"Then you killed him. No real incentive to return, was there?" He threw his bedroll on the ground and unrolled it with one hard swat. Frafnar was certain that if she could have found him after Raismus fell, she would have confronted him about it.

Aden jumped up and grabbed the waterskins. "I'll refill these and let you two catch up."

Frafnar's gaze followed the kit as he left the camp with the skins in one hand and a conjured ball of light in the other, to reveal his path through the shadows of dusk.

Ohn'na took a breath. "He's my first trainee. Can't you be nice?"

Frafnar shrugged. "If he's soon to become a knight, I'm sure he can handle it." He eyed Ohn'na closely. "Now who's becoming the protective old mentor?"

"Old?" Ohn'na made a face. "I'm just saying."

"If it will make you feel better, and stop the whining that's about to come, I'll go apologize, all right?" Despite all the time that had passed, she hadn't changed.

Ohn'na smiled. "It would indeed."

It didn't take Frafnar long to find the nearby river, located only a few yards from their camp. The kit had discovered a small inlet with few rocks and a lot of compact sand. There was a large rock at the edge of the fast-moving current with the water spilling over it. Nearby and undetected, Frafnar leaned against a tree. He watched as Aden removed his boots, rolled up his pant legs, and examined the area carefully before venturing out on the riverbank. He headed to the rock, but had to extinguish his light to properly fill the water skins.

Frafnar chose to remain inconspicuous for the time being. He closed his eyes while he listened to Aden's movements and took this opportunity to search deep within. Somehow they shared a connection, a bond he couldn't explain. Now that they were closer, he was sure that Ohn'na wasn't the one he'd reached but the trainee. *Why? Why him?* Was it a result of his power, or was this man's emotions leaving him vulnerable? Had the demose inspired it and was pretending otherwise? Frafnar eyes shot open to silence his questions. Too many possibilities, and until he had more insight it was a waste of time to speculate.

A thought occurred to him as Aden neared the edge of the fast water to fill the waterskins. He heard the demose whispering it at the edge of his consciousness. Just one little push and the kit would be cast downriver, outside the safety zone. The draquor could finish the job. In the meantime, he could tell Ohn'na that Aden had disappeared. He shook off the idea, though, knowing the knight wouldn't believe him, and right now he didn't need another enemy. At times, the woman seemed unguarded, but Frafnar knew her mind was as sharp as a newly forged blade. He clenched his fists. No, he would need the others to get out of this. Why had he even considered the alternative? But he knew the answer, imagining the malicious grin of the demose.

For now, he reined in his power ord limited his use of it around the others, uncertain how the knight and her kit would react to the dark gifts he possessed. In light of the draquor's ability to sense magic, Frafnar's restraint didn't seem to alarm the others. In fact, they understood the necessity and mimicked his behavior. The creatures would have difficulty pinpointing their location because of this, but would use their exceptional hunting and tracking skills to find them eventually.

Still unaware of his company, Aden did something Frafnar hadn't expected. When the kit removed his clothing, Frafnar almost gave himself away, but managed to stifle the laugh. This was no time to take a bath! Here he was, washing away when danger was on their heels—but then again, they were safe for the time being, so why not? Keenly aware of the state of his own body, Frafnar agreed that maybe it wasn't such a bad idea.

He heard Aden enter the water, and the moon peeked out from the clouds. The water came up to Aden's waist while more poured from above the rock. The kit wet his hair as the liquid ran down his back and followed the smooth and slightly muscular chest. Droplets clung to Aden's skin where the water didn't fall, sometimes connecting and dripping down together. It looked so refreshing that Frafnar considered jumping in himself, but decided to give Aden his privacy. He knew his presence wouldn't be welcomed since they hadn't started off on the best of terms. He'd come to apologize only to satisfy Ohn'na's whim, but the timing was bad. She would have to understand that. Frafnar took a step to leave, but his foot found a dry limb. *Crack.*

The kit whirled in Frafnar's direction. "Who's there?"

Aden used magic to brighten the area, but Frafnar easily escaped into the shadows and headed back to camp. He didn't have to wait long before Aden returned as well.

"Where's Ohn'na?" Aden asked when he arrived.

Frafnar had found a comfortable spot against a tree, and he sat with his hands behind his head. "She said she'd take first watch." He then stood, making a point of noticing Aden's drying hair. "I think I will go wash up too."

"Be careful," Aden called after him, "I heard something back there. Might be something dangerous."

Frafnar grinned to himself. *In a manner of speaking, it was.*

Aden tossed and turned in his sleep as the dreams claimed him again. He saw the silhouette of a man standing before the keepers during a public meeting, but he recognized Frafnar's voice.

"I'm merely suggesting we consider what the demose could offer. If we can use their power and block their control..."

Keeper Jormus jumped from her seat. *"We are not Remnents!"*

There was a flash and events skipped to a private conversation between Frafnar and Keeper Aera Nannelle, and the old dwarf spoke. *"It must be your orc blood..."* There was another flash. *"Easier to be corrupted..."*

There was a third flash and the vision returned to Frafnar during the public session at the citadel.

Keeper Nannelle declared the final decision. *"We cannot allow you to become a knight."*

Frafnar turned sharply on his heels and marched out of sight.

Aden awoke with a start. Bolting upright, he was relieved

to be in his bedroll with Frafnar sleeping nearby. That was until he saw the half-orc's eyes open.

"It was you!" Aden pointed straight at him.

"What are you talking about?" Frafnar asked.

But Aden wouldn't be fooled. "The dreams."

"I can't control what you dream about." Frafnar lay back down and tossed the blanket back over himself.

"What is it? What's wrong?" Ohn'na charged into camp from the trees, her weapon drawn and ready.

"Apparently your kit had a nightmare," Frafnar managed through a yawn.

Ohn'na questioned Aden, concern written all over her face. "Is this true? I heard you yell. Is everything all right?"

Not really wanting to get into the details of it, he waved her off. "Yes. Yes, it was nothing. I will take watch now." Aden hurried away in the direction where the guardian had entered the camp. He didn't know why it upset him so much, that Frafnar was the one he was connecting with. Was it because he'd left the Order due to his extreme ideals? Or was it because Aden could empathize with the feelings of being denied knighthood after working so hard for it. He needed some distance, some time to mull it over.

"What's with him?" He heard Ohn'na ask.

"Just a bad dream."

7

―――――

IN THE RAIN

"Just like old times."

―――――――――――――――――――――――――――――――――

The full moon had already slipped down to the horizon when an uneasiness crept over him. The sky was still dark, but the dim light of morning was slowly bringing the world back into view. The smell of rain was heavy in the air as dark clouds rolled in.

Aden squatted. All his senses were on alert, his muscles rigid and tense. The area was too quiet; even the birds refused to sing. The wind was picking up and it blew across Aden's face, sending chills down his spine. He would have thought nothing about the silence, perhaps blaming it on the approaching storm, if it wasn't for the tight knot in his stomach. He saw the light of the camp from his perch and was relieved that the others had roused from their slumber.

He dropped from his vantage point, heading to meet up with his companions. He knelt as he hit the ground to absorb the fall. Movement from the corner of his eye warned him of the impending danger. He saw the creature, even through the shadows of early morning. It was about the height of two men, reminding Aden of a yeti, a large humanoid creature with long gray hair covering its entire body. He wondered how such large creatures could be so silent.

Aden stood and went for his weapon, but before his fingers reached their mark, a blast of energy knocked him off his feet. He flew through the air and hit a nearby tree, forcing the breath from his lungs. Aden gasped, but before he could recover he saw the draquor's legs before him. With astute instinct, Aden dropped a shoulder and let his body roll to the side, barely avoiding the claws that had tried to grab him. As he pulled his sword free, the creature caught him with a backhand. He was flung back and his weapon slipped from his grasp.

The draquor lifted a massive foot and tried to crush him while he lay dazed. Aden instinctively rolled to the side again, narrowly avoiding the creature's feet as it continued to stomp after him. Aden maintained his momentum until he managed to plant a leg under him and sprang up, making the draquor hesitate. He ran two steps then climbed the creature, one leg on its knee and the other on its hip. He swung his foot to score a hit, hoping to stun it long enough to retrieve his blade. But the creature was ready for him. The draquor grabbed his leg, swung him around, and let go. Aden threw out his arms to protect himself and crashed through the tree branches. He spotted his weapon while landing in a roll, and took it. He stood, and sensing his adversary right on his heels, he swung a large cutting sweep. The sharp blade easily sliced through the resistance, splitting the creature in half. The draquor's body disintegrated, the dust flying in the wind. Aden took a moment to catch his breath.

They are coming. Frafnar tried to ignore the feeling—certain the draquor wouldn't dare set foot here—but the notion plagued him even in sleep. His dreams replayed one of his encounters with the draquor, and the information he had extracted from its mind. *Once every cycle... the brightest face... the sacred land could be scoured...*

The full moon! Frafnar woke instantly. He sensed the danger now, uncertain of how he had overlooked this detail. There was no time to berate himself, though—they had to get away from here! He found Ohn'na, who still slept nearby. *Of course.* He flicked the end of her nose. "Ohn'na!"

"Do it again, Var'rune."

Frafnar paused and arched an eyebrow. He placed a hand on her shoulder, and with frightening speed and strength, she hooked his arm and pulled him to the ground. She held his arms and her knee pinned him in the back while his face was planted in the dirt—a reminder of how defensive her unconscious was when she slept.

Ohn'na's eyes opened, and she immediately let him go. "Oh, sorry... you weren't trying something naughty, were you,

Fraf?" Her sly grin dropped when she saw his face. "What is it?"

"They're coming," Frafnar whispered, while eyeing the edges of camp, expecting the creatures to jump out at any moment. He took a heartbeat to stretch his arms out after Ohn'na's brutal hold on them.

She must have recognized the tension in his words because she held her questions, and hurried to pack whatever supplies she could while Frafnar kept a lookout. She hoisted one of the bags on her shoulders and handed the other to him. "Aden should be on his way back to camp."

"If he's smart, he'll run far from this place. Either way, we can't wait fo—"

Frafnar sighed. They'd run out of time; the draquor had surrounded them. He positioned himself against Ohn'na's back and heard her draw her weapon. Together, they had a chance. Frafnar looked down the length of his old blade, the one he'd forged while still a kit in the Order. The violet crystal within the hilt shone bright, driving back the darkness as if being called into service once more brought it joy. He hadn't used it since the day he'd left the Order, the day he had its partner reforged from dagger to blade. The sword the draquor had stolen when he'd first encountered them. The feeling of the old weapon was comforting somehow, and it strengthened his resolve. He clenched the hilt tightly, his confidence unwavering.

"Just like old times." Ohn'na grinned despite the situation, a glint of excitement in her eyes.

Water sizzled on the nearby fire as light rain began to fall and thunder rumbled far away. In unison, the draquor roared and charged. Frafnar met their ferocity with calm focus, his blade at the ready.

Just like old times.

Aden ran, dodging and outrunning the draquor that tried to stop him. He used magic to quicken his movements, the falling rain moving slower than normal. He heard the loud roars up ahead and surged forward. He stopped dead in his tracks when the camp came into view; Ohn'na and Frafnar were surrounded. Slashing and stabbing with their swords, they held back waves of creatures by working together and covering each other's vulnerabilities.

As he paused to consider how he was going to assist them, Aden was tackled to the ground. The draquor tried to use its mass to crush him, but Aden achieved freedom with a quick thrust of his blade. The creature disintegrated and Aden breathed again.

At the same moment, he saw a dart graze Ohn'na's leg and break her rhythm. The draquor took the advantage and worked together to form a powerful spell. The magic pushed past their prey's defenses and threw Frafnar clear from the ring of enemies. He landed on his back, and a pair of the creatures jumped after him, but he was able to cut down one of them in mid-jump. The remaining beast was moments from landing on top of him when he managed to hold the weight, through force of will alone. The creature hung in the air a few feet above its victim, but lowered a finger's length every few heartbeats. Aden rushed to help, and the creature vanished after his blade emerged from its midsection. Frafnar scrambled to his feet.

"Ohn'na!" Aden called when he caught sight of her.

The guardian was doing amazingly well for herself, but another dart struck her arm and the creatures were over-whelming her. "Go! Run! *Run!*" Ohn'na yelled before she was lost in the throng of enemies.

"No!" Aden watched the draquor rally to their prize and took a step to go after her, but Frafnar caught his wrist.

"We need to go. Now! Before the beasts are upon us."

Aden barely heard him over the rumble of thunder, but he yanked his arm away. Frafnar blocked his path, and a fevered desperation overrode all his senses. Aden lifted his blade. "Get. Out. Of. My. Way. You said it was safe. We trusted you!"

"Are you going to attack me?" Frafnar asked with a calm Aden hadn't expected.

Aden blinked the rain out of his eyes as he searched for the answer. "I must save her. I can't simply run away."

"She gave you an order. Run. Will you defy her?"

"Yes." Aden glared at Frafnar; he didn't have to explain himself to this half-orc. He took a step to maneuver around his obstacle, expecting Frafnar to let him go.

"I can't let you do that."

Aden barely managed to block the attack as Frafnar struck relentlessly, and it was pure instinct that kept the half-orc at bay. Swords clashed as the rain poured, the clang echoing the flashes of lightning and rumbles of thunder.

"What are you doing?" Aden yelled. "Ohn'na is—"

"You want to throw yourself to those fiends? You fool."

"We don't have time for this!" Aden tried to break away from Frafnar, but the half-orc's assaults were unrelenting.

After a meager minute or so, a horde of draquor roared upon them. Aden and Frafnar simultaneously disengaged from each other to defend themselves. The sheer number of creatures gradually pushed them back to the ridge of a steep hill. Aden saw the landscape roll out far beneath them. They did their best to keep the creatures back, but it was clear they were losing the battle. Aden knew his end was near when one of the draquor disarmed him with a spell. It seized his weapon and lunged at him with it. There was a strong tug at his back, and Aden fell from the ridge. Before his mind could register what had happened, he found himself sliding down the hill, water and mud moving with him. His head connected with a rock on the way down, which enveloped his world in complete darkness.

Aden slowly became aware of the rain. It fell lightly now, and the sound was soothing to his throbbing head. Then the memories of sliding down the hill came flooding back to him, as well as the pain in his muscles. He groaned as he tried to move, his body was stiff. Nothing was broken, at least.

"I see you're finally awake."

Aden, covered with mud from head to toe, had to wipe his

face before he spotted Frafnar. The half-orc looked just as battered as Aden felt. "What? What happened?"

"When that draquor was about to gut you, I pulled you off the edge as I leaped. Then we had a fun slide down the ridge." Frafnar indicated the supply pack that lay nearby. "Who would have thought that would save me from the rough drop?"

Aden rubbed the lump on his head. "Thanks a lot."

Frafnar ignored the sarcasm and continued. "The draquor were still following, but fortunately the river was nearby. I carried you to the river and found a hollowed out log that swept us away from those relentless hounds."

Aden was silent. He had saved him? "But you attacked me."

"Yes." Frafnar looked him straight in the eye. "You weren't thinking clearly. Your emotions were clouding your better judgment. My intention was to distract you."

"We could have killed each other!" Aden tried to yell, but his dry voice cracked.

Frafnar tossed him a waterskin. "Perhaps, but you'll have to fight better than that to kill me."

Aden was a bit irritated for having owed his life—multiple times—to this half-orc. Frafnar reeked of arrogance. Aden drank the water and stood carefully, feeling every muscle complain with the effort. He searched his pocket and was relieved to find the verge stone still there. He used it to reach out to Ohn'na, but she didn't answer. He began walking. He didn't know how, but he was going to find her.

"Where are you going?"

"To look for Ohn'na."

Frafnar pinched the bridge of his nose as he shook his head, his annoyance plain to see. "You are tired and weak, and you're still trying and save her? You can barely walk. Even together we would be hard-pressed to defeat creatures that feel no fatigue, have no need to eat or sleep."

"I'll find a way." Unmistakably Frafnar was about to say more when he blurted out, "I am going, with or without you."

"Look." Frafnar had caught up. Aden heard the anger in his tone, but he hadn't expected Frafnar to grab him by the throat and slam him against the nearest tree, pinning him there. "I will hold you here until you come to your senses. Ohn'na's gone."

Aden slumped. "I... I can't lose... another..." His eyes teared up, unable to hide the grief.

Frafnar must have recognized the agony in his eyes, for he released him, then stepped back. "I said she was *gone*, not dead."

And with that, Frafnar slung the supply pack over his shoulder and continued walking, heading in the direction of the mountains. Aden stood there, his stare locked on Frafnar's back.

"What?"

"Would you have left me there?"

Ohn'na will be safe until the draquor take her to their elders and sacrifice her to their god. To minimize the risk to their prisoner, her captors will avoid the mountains by taking a longer path. We should catch up to them if we cut through the peaks," Frafnar explained as they made their way through the wilderness.

Aden was relieved beyond words. They would save Ohn'na; he refused to consider any other alternative. He'd tried to reach her through the verge stone again, but there was still no answer. He only hoped Frafnar was right about the draquor.

The river had swept them closer to the mountains during their escape. It was about midday when they came across a small creek and decided to rest. They had maintained a grueling pace toward the peaks, and Aden welcomed the breather. He collapsed by the water as the strain of their ordeal took its toll. Although Aden hated the idea of stopping, he couldn't deny his exhaustion. The draquor wouldn't need to rest, but he knew Ohn'na would slow the creatures as much as possible.

With a grunt, Frafnar removed the pack from his shoulders. "Wait here while I hunt for food—it's important we preserve our strength. There's no point in pushing ourselves to our very limits if we are too weak to save Ohn'na. We need to hurry, but must also be ready to face the draquor." He tossed Aden some soggy rations from the supply pack and took some for himself before disappearing into the wilderness.

It baffled Aden where Frafnar found the energy for hunting, but the rumbling of his stomach brought his attention back to the food. He ate hungrily despite the bland taste and grainy texture of the rations, thankful something filled him. He repositioned himself to face the direction his companion had disappeared. Aden was worried about Ohn'na, but now that they had a plan to save her, his mind drifted back to what had happened. He was embarrassed that Frafnar had witnessed his emotional outburst, even though he didn't comment on it. The pain of losing Cormell was still too fresh, and if he'd lost Ohn'na too, that just might break him.

And what about Frafnar? Ohn'na had been responsible for the death of his mentor... but had he moved on from that? Had he even cared, or was he only angry that the keepers had withheld his knighthood? Frafnar had allied himself with them so he could leave this place, but would he turn on them once they escaped? Despite Ohn'na's feelings about her old friend, Aden wasn't so sure.

He remembered the demose wasn't in control of Frafnar now, but how long would that last? And what about his orc heritage; what was the story behind it? He didn't know of any orc members in the Order, since most revered and served the demons. Also, they didn't have an ounce of magical potential, let alone gritt. Although, Frafnar could probably attribute his gifts to his mixed blood.

Aden refilled a waterskin, then let the water pour over his head. For now, they all needed each other, so what was to come would have to be dealt with later. He only hoped he wouldn't have to battle the draquor *and* the half-orc as well. He lay in the grass and waited for Frafnar to return. The clouds began to break a little, and the sun peeked out from behind them. Aden tried to dry himself in the light while his eyelids struggled to stay open despite his uneasy thoughts. The sun warmed him and gave him some comfort.

Frafnar hunted and tossed their dinner into the pack. He wasn't certain if Aden would find it peculiar that he'd taken the bag with him, but the trainee hadn't mentioned it.

Frafnar knew the draquor were stalking them. Several had managed to cross the river, had found their trail, and now were hiding their presence and biding their time. If he focused hard enough, he sensed them nearby, if ever so vaguely. He didn't want their pursuers warning the others, or worse, to capture them. Frafnar left the camp to tempt the creatures to attack with Aden there alone. He watched from his vantage point on the slope of a hill to give the draquor the time they needed to surround the kit. As he kept an eye out for enemies, a plan formed in his mind.

Aden was on the verge of sleep when his instincts warned him of danger. He sprang to his feet and ignored the sting as something grazed his hand. He counted seven of the creatures, and his hand automatically went to draw his sword. As he realized his weapon was missing—likely in some grisly draquor treasure trove by now—he did the only thing that came to mind. Aden spun on his heels and ran. Some may have called it cowardly, but certain death or capture awaited him otherwise.

Two of the creatures that had circled around behind him, but he continued his charge toward them. The same direction in which Frafnar had gone. The half-orc sprang up and used surprise to his advantage as he neatly carved the two creatures with his blade.

"This way!" Frafnar called and led the way.

The draquor were large, but they were equally fast. Aden struggled to stay ahead of them. Frafnar led them up a hill, to an entrance of a cave. With the creatures close on their heels, they rushed into the darkness. Frafnar mumbled words of power, and magic runes glowed on the walls. Moments after they passed, the explosions caused dirt to loosen from above.

This however didn't seem to deter the creatures behind them. Aden could already see the light from the other side of the cave. Frafnar continued to strategically place runes, and with each subsequent explosion, the earth shifted. Their footfalls echoed off the walls of the cave, mixing with the rumble of falling rock. When they neared the exit, Frafnar stepped to the side to allow Aden to run past and then used his power to create a massive force wave, pushing in all directions. The floor shook as the walls fractured, and when the ceiling collapsed, he jumped out of the way before it crushed him. His stunt knocked the draquor off their feet, while blocks of rock crumbled on top of them.

Aden gasped from the sprint and the cloud of dust that spewed through the air while Frafnar took a moment to lay on the grass. They had succeeded, and the draquor would pursue them no more. Once he'd recovered his breath, Aden noticed that they had entered a valley. "Where are we?"

"We are near the base of the mountains, which will lead us straight to where the draquor are taking Ohn'na. The cave was made from the snowmelts and finalized my plan perfectly." Frafnar pointed to the peaks in the distance.

Aden froze on the spot. "Plan?"

"Yes. If I hadn't left you alone, the draquor would still be hounding us. We couldn't save Ohn'na with them at our backs."

"Wait a minute." Aden shook his head, trying to understand. "Let me get this straight. You used me as bait, and you never told me?"

"It had to be done."

Aden clenched his jaw shut, holding back a slew of curses. He didn't like being used, especially when he was purposely left in the dark. He began to leave but had to suppress a groan when he put pressure on his leg. His limb felt prickly, as if it had fallen asleep. His right hand felt the same and he shook it, trying to get the blood flowing.

Before he could react, Frafnar grabbed his wrist to inspect the problem. "You're injured."

Aden tried to yank his hand away, but the half-orc's grip was firm. "It's just a scratch."

"Sit," Frafnar commanded. "You'll be useless to me if we don't fix this now."

Blood had soaked into his pant leg and now Aden couldn't take a step without severely limping. Impatient, the half-orc clutched Aden's arm and, with little effort, put him on his backside.

"You could at least ask nicely."

Frafnar examined the wounds closer. The cut in his leg was deeper than Aden had thought. With all the adrenaline pumping through him, the injury felt minor.

"It appears that the draquor marred you with their darts. You're lucky it is merely a flesh wound." Frafnar searched in his belt pouches.

Aden chuckled. "Or what? Would you have left me there?"

When Frafnar didn't answer, Aden wondered if the half-orc really would have abandoned him.

"Here." Frafnar shoved a small vial in Aden's hand. "Their weapons are coated with a paralyzing poison, and even a small cut could disable you. This antidote will take some time to cure it."

Aden opened the top and swallowed the liquid, almost gagging. It was foul, like nothing he had ever tasted before. He sputtered and wiped his mouth. "How do you know all this?" Aden managed through another cough. "And where did you get this?"

Frafnar remained silent and turned his head in the direction of the mountains. *Fine, keep your secrets*, Aden thought. He stood up but winced when he put any pressure on his leg. The pain and the numbness were slowing him. He tried to move faster but ended up almost falling, had Frafnar not steadied him. Aden was a little apprehensive when the man unsheathed his blade.

"We will never make it like this, something must be done."

Ohn'na found herself being bound and carried most of the time. At the moment, the draquor had stopped to let her relieve herself, eat, and drink. She didn't know why they kept her alive, but she assumed there was a reason. They wouldn't have healed her injuries and forced her to swallow some Divine awful swill if they didn't have a plan in mind.

What had happened to Aden and Frafnar? She hoped the draquor hadn't killed them, but if they'd been captured they'd be joining her soon. Every time she tried to use magic, the creatures would block her efforts. She'd heard the ping of her verge stone, but before she could answer, one of the creatures grabbed it. The draquor had snapped the stone in half, as easily as one might a twig.

She sighed. Her first mission with her first trainee hadn't gone the way she'd expected. When another cluster of creatures joined her group without either of her companions, Ohn'na didn't know if she should be relieved or concerned. The leaders of the two parties spoke quietly among themselves. She understood their speech when they ordered her to eat and drink, but now they kept their voices low and spoke in their ancient tongue. None of the draquor were paying her any attention, so she tried to slip away. She crept on her hands and knees, until a sharp object poked her in the back. She turned to face a draquor, unmistakably angry and pointing a dangerous blade at her. Aden's blade. With one glance, she knew her trainee was alive. The blue gem and silvery steel glinted lively in the sunlight.

Ohn'na held up her hands in surrender. "All right... all right."

9

RESCUE

"We just had to take the scenic route."

This *is so embarrassing,* Aden thought. To ensure they made it in time, Frafnar had insisted on carrying him. At first Aden thought he was joking, but soon learned otherwise. Before they set out, Frafnar had cut strips of fabric from Aden's cloak to bind his wounds.

So now they traveled, the supply pack in place on him, and Aden secured to Frafnar's back with his arms around the half-orc's neck and his legs held by strong muscular arms. Frafnar used a fortitude spell to help him, making the weight lighter and his strides longer. The sun was still high in the sky, so they hoped to reach the end of the valley by nightfall.

Aden rested his chin on his arm, looking ahead. There wasn't much to see in the valley consisting of mostly grasses and its various grazers, which scattered as they approached. The lull of the rhythmic movement sent his thoughts wandering as Frafnar whisked him across the valley. He still had many questions, but he debated whether to push for the answers. Frafnar hadn't been too open about anything, and Aden wasn't sure the half-orc would be honest with him. This internal debate continued until they neared the edge of the valley.

Frafnar had reached his limit by the time they approached their destination. He unloaded Aden and dropped to the grass. The sun was well on its way to setting now, and the light bathed everything in a golden glow. The sky was a mixture of pink and purples on the horizon, and fluffy clouds floated silently by. It would be dark soon. Aden, mindful of Frafnar's fatigue, had already started making a fire. He knew they would need the heat to last through the night, an insight gleaned from the chill in the wind as it swept over them from the mountaintops. As he worked, his limp improved. It confirmed the potion was working to counteract the poison. Aden opened the supply pack for rations, but what he found inside made him jump back.

"What is *that*?"

"Dinner."

Aden reached for a stick and poked the animal. Once he had determined that the creature was indeed dead, he turned to Frafnar. "It's been in there this whole time? It's probably not fit to eat anymore, if edible it ever was."

"Bring it here," Frafnar responded, annoyance thick in his

tone, "I will deal with it. You should be thankful; neither of us is in any shape to hunt, especially in the dark."

Aden gladly handed it over and continued to feed the fire while Frafnar prepared the food. It didn't take long for the meat to cook, and as Aden handled a small piece he mumbled, "We'll probably get food poisoning."

"If you die, I'll be sure to send Ohn'na my regards... and congratulations." Frafnar licked his fingers as Aden rolled his eyes. "I would just as soon not share if I didn't need your strength for the coming battle," Frafnar added.

Aden slowly peeked back in the pack and realized they only had enough rations for one meal. Maybe he should be grateful; he had to admit that the meat tasted better than expected. He refused to say it, though.

Silence fell between them then, each in his own thoughts. Aden once again considered if he should trouble Frafnar with his questions. This indecisiveness continued until he blurted it out. "Why did you save me?"

There was a pause. "What?"

Aden felt the knot in his stomach. Ultimately, as hard as it was to ask, he had to know. "Back there. Before. You saved me when you could have easily escaped on your own. I always thought those who joined with the demose despise weakness."

A sly grin formed on Frafnar's lips. "Has that been on your mind this whole time?"

Aden didn't respond, only patiently waited for his answer. Frafnar's eyes gazed into his and made Aden want to look away, but he forced himself not to.

Frafnar shrugged. "The demose is always whispering dark

things. At times it becomes hard to separate my own thoughts from its murmurs..." But Frafnar quickly changed the mood of the conversation. "And why do you seem to care so much? Not starting to like me... are you?"

The weight of what the man had shared caught Aden off guard, but his stubbornness manifested itself in light of Frafnar's question. He refused to answer, and Frafnar had an amused expression on his face as Aden knelt to put down the bedroll instead.

The dim glow on the horizon was now all that remained of the setting sun, and Aden tightened his tattered cloak to try and fend off the cool night air. He was startled when he felt Frafnar lie next to him. "Aren't you going to keep watch?"

"Be my guest. But I, for one, am tired. We should be safe here." Frafnar removed his cloak and laid it over both of them.

"Where have I heard that before?"

Frafnar's eyes narrowed. "What was that?"

"Nothing." He took off his own cloak and laid it on top of Frafnar's. It was in shreds, but the additional layer was better than nothing. He wrapped his arms around himself in an attempt to trap as much heat as possible. He was disappointed, having hoped that Frafnar would explain more than he had. At the same time, he was surprised that the man had shared anything at all. But before he could ponder on it further, he fell into the soothing nothingness of sleep.

Frafnar lay on his back with his hands behind his head and

eyes cast toward the stars. As tired as he was, his mind raced, denying him the sleep he desperately needed. A light snow fell from a cloud passing over, each flake visible in the moonlight.

Would you have left me there? What unnerved him wasn't the question itself, but rather the unspoken answer. If he hadn't needed Aden, and the kit had sustained more serious injuries, Frafnar would have left him. This line of thinking troubled him. It had been some time since he'd been around other members of the Order. Wandering the darkness with the demose had made it seem longer. What had happened to him? What *was* happening to him? He no longer walked that fine line; he had fallen, even if ever so slightly. *It was necessary*, he tried to convince himself. Any sort of slip and he'd be killed. His eyes fell on Aden, sleeping soundly next to him. He had to harden, be immune to either influence. Just when his resolve was the strongest, it shattered with one tiny act of innocence.

Aden rolled over and put his arm on Frafnar. "Warm," the trainee mumbled in his sleep.

Another question still hung in the air. *Why did you save me?*

When they finally reached their destination, Ohn'na couldn't tell where the wilderness ended and the settlement began. Ruins were visible here and there, but most were covered with vines and foliage. A single, solitary temple was the only remarkable structure within the area.

Ohn'na was roughly pushed to the base of the steps that

led up to a platform, where the elders stood waiting. Uncountable numbers of draquor stood behind her and her captors, roaring and grunting. The mob silenced when one elder emerged from the rest, arms raised. He took a step to the side, and revealed the object behind him, making the crowd roar again. To Ohn'na it looked like a mirror, but shimmered and rippled like the surface of water when the elder passed a clawed hand over the smudged glass. It was a portal. This was probably how the Remnent had escaped long ago. However, it didn't appear like it would be Ohn'na's salvation. When the view of what was beyond came into focus, it depicted a fiery surface. The guardian knew she needed more sun, but not an inferno.

If you guys are still out there, now would be the time, Ohn'na thought, perspiration sliding down her temple. She was shoved forward.

Why Frafnar seemed in a foul mood the next morning was beyond Aden, and he wisely left the man to his brooding. Now they looked down at the congregation of draquor, with Ohn'na in tow.

"That building should contain the source that sustains these creatures. I will go through the back, while you create a diversion and save Ohn'na. Keep them occupied for as long as you can." Frafnar took stock of the number of draquor that were down there while he explained his plan.

"Might I remind you, I lost my weapon," Aden whispered back.

"I'm sure you'll think of something."

"But I—wait!" Aden called as loudly as he dared, but Frafnar had already gone. "Great."

Fortunately, Frafnar had no intention of leaving him without help. Aden watched as he made a detour and conjured an illusion of himself behind the draquor then headed to do his own part. Frafnar's copy used the few abilities it was granted by its maker, and threw conjured lightning into the mob of creatures. Sparks flew between the draquor, but they turned in unison and roared at the intrusion, shaking off the energy as one would a cloak. After succeeding in getting their attention, the illusion retreated.

A creature held up Aden's weapon and motioned for the crowd to charge after the intruder. Ohn'na took her chance and used a force of magic to yank the blade from the draquor's grasp. The creature was faster than the knight had anticipated, though. Even as the sword slipped from its claws, it used its own abilities to draw it back. The weapon hung in the air, moving slightly, back and forth between them.

Aden enchanted himself to quicken his pace, sprinting so fast in his desperation to make it in time that everything stopped. When he arrived at Ohn'na's side, the guardian and the draquor remained at a standstill. Aden's weapon hung between them and, as soon as his fingertips touched the hilt, time seemed to catch up with him. Aden sliced at the creature, disbelief evident in its eyes as it fell. He cut Ohn'na from her bonds then dealt with the draquor stragglers.

Ohn'na reclaimed her own blade that had fallen to the ground when the creature had disappeared, and helped him. "Cutting it a bit close, aren't we?" She spoke over the chaos and was clearly relieved to see him.

"Oh, you know"—Aden ducked away from darts that were fired at him—"we just had to take the scenic route."

Nearby, Frafnar entered the rear entrance as the distraction succeeded in pulling the guards away. As he stepped through the doorway, the familiar sense of dark magic surrounded him. The circular room was empty except for a round artifact that stood on a pedestal in the center. It glowed, different shades of red swirling in its depths. He sensed this was what sustained the draquor, and he approached it but stopped when he heard movement from behind. He turned to face a creature who wielded a dark sword. Frafnar felt a surge of anger. It was his blade, stolen from him when he'd first encountered the race, and he would reclaim it. The draquor wielding his weapon was one of the elders, malice and contempt dominating its features.

"Undoubtedly you learned all you could from your master before you betrayed him." Frafnar spoke, studying his enemy.

The draquor only answered him with a roar, and then lunged.

Ohn'na and her trainee were confronted and surrounded by several elder draquor. The creatures used their powers to create an energy similar to the one that had nearly caught them in the sky. The elders positioned themselves away from the pair, attacking from a safe distance. Other draquor that realized Frafnar's illusion wasn't a threat, now gathered to complete the circle around them. The pair fought together, back-to-back, defending any exposed openings in their defense.

When three elders joined their beams together and concentrated on Ohn'na, Aden sacrificed a grazing blow to save her from the assault. He used both hands to hold the energy at bay while the beams pushed him back a few feet through the dirt. Ohn'na nodded her thanks, and when more streams of magical energy tried to take Aden while he was preoccupied, she blocked both beam and draquor attack alike.

"All right, Frafnar," Aden said, "anytime now."

Just when it looked like they would be overrun, all the draquor fell silent and their attacks ceased. They stood for a few moments until their bodies disintegrated into the wind. Both Aden and Ohn'na bent over, catching their breath, and Frafnar staggered from the structure and met them.

"What took you so long?" Aden straightened and put pressure on his minor injury.

"I had my own problems to deal with." Then a smirk tugged at the corners of Frafnar's mouth. "I can't save you *all* the time."

A dismissive wave was the only response Aden seemed willing to give.

Ohn'na laughed. "I imagine I'm in for some interesting stories."

The three then moved to the portal where Ohn'na had almost met her demise. Frafnar waved his hand over the portal so it no longer displayed the burning surface, and now revealed a shadowed hallway.

Frafnar studied the visage. "This portal is likely how the Remnent escaped. The power has been greatly drained, but enough remains for our use. I have already set the destinations. I presume you'll want to update the keepers on what has happened here."

"Yes, thank you." Ohn'na then paused a moment. "You aren't coming with us?"

"I have my own path now, but I'm sure we'll meet again."

Frafnar lifted his hood over his head. "Tell the Council, the darkness is on their doorstep. It will show itself soon." Then he placed the mask on his face.

As Frafnar stepped over the threshold, Aden cried out. "Wait!" His arm passed through the surface, but when he tried to retract his limb, the portal pulled him through instead.

"Aden?" Ohn'na stood in disbelief when she realized she was now alone. The view within the portal transformed and showed the familiar halls of Longshield Citadel.

Aden appeared in the dimly lit hallway, and a dark sensation hit him like a blow. Frafnar stopped a few paces ahead and turned. Aden backed up, trying to feel for the portal behind him, but was met only by the cold stone of the wall. "I-I just wanted to say thank you... where are we?"

Frafnar approached and stood before him, moving in close to whisper in his ear. The way the mask changed Frafnar's voice made Aden's skin crawl. "You shouldn't have followed me."

A hard head-butt knocked Aden to the ground. No sooner had he fallen than a group of men came running.

"Captain Armastus! Zeffron said you were dead!"

"Did he?" Frafnar's words were cold as steel. "I'm sure he'll soon wish I was."

"Sir, what of this one?" The senior member of the group indicated Aden on the floor.

"Secure him in my quarters. I will deal with him later. Right now, I have a score to settle."

The men lifted Aden to his feet and dragged him along. His eyes opened slightly, one last time. He saw Frafnar walk away down a dark corridor, his cloak swaying behind him. Then it all faded.

10

AN ANCHOR

"Something to hold on to."

A meeting of the captains had been called. Frafnar was one of the dozen kneeling figures, awaiting the arrival of their leader. The ghostly image before them became more visible, and a familiar hooded woman appeared above the communication rune.

"Zeffron, what is the meaning of this? I was informed that Frafnar was dead, but now he stands before me. Explain this."

Frafnar was no stranger to this voice, as were all who obeyed it. Their leader never spoke to them in person, always from a distance. Always safe. But he was getting closer. If she expected her followers to remain loyal, she couldn't always stay far.

The other captain next to Frafnar shifted uncertainly.

"Mistress, I believed he'd perished while surveying the area you'd ordered searched. For the time being, I thought it would be wise to plan ahead before losing any more men..."

As much as Frafnar enjoyed seeing the man squirm, he wanted to end this quickly. He'd barely had enough time to clean himself of the sweat and dirt of his ordeal before being summoned for the meeting. He desired to deal with Zeffron personally, and it took little effort to find the anger he felt toward the man.

"Mistress, if I may? We have lost precious time, but what we gained in return will be well worth it." Frafnar revealed the oval artifact that had kept the draquor alive.

The leader eyed the item and was silent for a moment, then spoke. "You've done well. Leave it with my agent. As for you, Zeffron, I'm very displeased, and know if I hadn't need of you..." She left the thought unfinished, leaving the gruesome details to their imagination. "Never fail me again."

"Yes, Mistress."

"Now, prepare your men. The details of your next mission will be given soon. Be ready." Her transparent figure faded, leaving the captains to their duties.

As the others filed out of the room, Frafnar was approached by the same goblin he'd noticed in previous meetings. The creature watched him and held out his ghostly hand. Frafnar dropped the artifact into the palm of the unusual extremity. The goblin's new hand could have only been the work of the Mistress, a testament to her power.

The creature nodded as he took the artifact. "Good work, *Captain*." He sent Frafnar one last sidelong look beneath the brim of his hat before he stepped away, leaving the others to their business.

Zeffron and Frafnar were the last to remain in the room. They eyed each other, both unrelenting. Zeffron circled slowly. "You should have died in the wilds where you belong. Your men are mine now."

Frafnar matched the man step for step. "I think the Mistress will understand if I kill you"—Frafnar smirked—"the failure that you are." He felt the anger hit him a moment before Zeffron attacked. Frafnar took a side step as the man sprang at him and scored a grazing cut to the captain's thigh. This seemed to only infuriate Zeffron more, who retaliated with vicious precision. They exchanged blows for a time until Zeffron stumbled and fell.

"What have you done to me?"

Frafnar paused to look at his blade. He saw a faint residue of poison, probably the very same which had been used on Aden. The draquor had been busy. Lucky for Frafnar, unfortunate for Zeffron. He stood over the captain and placed the tip of his sword on the man's chest.

"I knew you were a coward." Zeffron said, clearly afraid for his life, although he continued to taunt him. "Finish it! You'll wish I'd been the one to grant you death when the Mistress learns of this."

Frafnar hesitated but remained poised with his blade dangerously close when the demon whispered in his mind.

"Kill him..."

He certainly wanted to. With Zeffron out of the way, Frafnar could then seize his troops and wedge himself deeper into the ranks of the renegades. But he wasn't a murderer. And Zeffron had a point: the Mistress had banned any violence among them.

"Kill him!" the demose urged further, despite all logic.

No! Frafnar felt the demon push against his will, and he shoved back. It took everything he had to move his blade away from Zeffron. His control was slipping; he could feel it. The demose gained more and more influence every day, and the mask only magnified the demon's hold on him.

"Since the Mistress didn't see fit to kill you, I will let you live. For now." Frafnar had to force the words, then turned on his heels and left the man there. Through the ensuing curses Zeffron threw at him, the demose whispered its own remarks.

"You can't fight me forever. You will succumb."

Ohn'na stared at the sword in her hands. Aden's weapon. Left alone, Ohn'na had no choice but to return to Longshield Citadel with only the blade as her companion. The last time she had done this... her mentor had been defeated. It felt all too familiar.

She worried for Aden. As soon as her feet touched the floor of the citadel, she headed for the keepers' meeting chamber. Why would Frafnar have a message for the keepers? The more she thought about the situation, the greater her concern grew.

As she stepped into the room, she was only a little surprised to find Keeper Nannelle alone, staring out at the horizon. *How does she do that?* Ohn'na wondered. Nannelle was always there when she was needed, and somehow knew when she wanted a private conversation.

"Aden didn't come back with you." The old keeper spoke without turning to see who was there.

Ohn'na's shoulders slumped; she felt berated even though she knew the keeper wasn't laying blame, only making a statement. Ohn'na wasted no time in filling her in on what had happened. Nannelle listened in silence, neither commenting nor questioning.

"Frafnar left the Council a message," Ohn'na finished. "He said, 'The darkness is on our doorstep.' Keeper, what did he mean? What's going on?"

The older woman pressed her lips together—as she always did when deep in thought—before she spoke. "The knight's order... it was our order that threw him on a dangerous path."

Ohn'na's mind whirled in confusion, but she continued to listen.

"To infiltrate the ranks of the renegades, the keepers proposed that Frafnar join with a demon. They may have never trusted his loyalty otherwise. He had no friends or family, no one close to him. No anchor, something to hold on to. Nothing to fear losing. Frafnar was one of the few who could deal with a demose and fight its influence. He trained himself for this, to stay in that shadow between light and dark." Nannelle shook her head. "But it wasn't enough. Easy to be swept away in the current of hatred and revenge without realizing it. What he used to combat the darkness also pulled him in." She paused for a moment. "But despite that—albeit ever so slightly—I can feel his spark once again. If Aden was able to sense his turmoil from such a distance, and somehow aid him...”

With this enlightening information, Ohn'na completely understood. She also faced the window, finishing the thought in her mind. *Aden could indeed become powerful.*

“Frafnar sent us a warning,” Nannelle continued. “We must be ready.”

Aden paced the room. He tried the door but it was locked, immune to any spell he cast. His weapon was gone. He couldn't remember where he'd dropped it, but hopefully it wasn't gone for good. He had no idea where he was, or why he was here. The only thing he was certain of was the oppressive darkness that surrounded him. Clothes had been laid out for him, and with nothing to do other than wait, he took the opportunity to use the washbasin in the next room to clean up and dress.

His head still throbbed, but after washing and resting his body felt better. He forced himself to be still, crossing his legs and sitting on the bed rather than pacing back and forth. He remembered being pulled through the portal unexpectedly, seeing Frafnar, feeling the dark energy as he did now. What was the man involved with?

Aden struggled to still his mind, without much success. Then the door opened and he jumped to his feet when Frafnar entered, followed by a pair of men.

"You may leave." Frafnar turned to his subordinates. "Ensure the others are prepared for the mission."

Once the men closed the door behind them, Frafnar put down his mask and Aden took this opportunity to question him. "What—?"

Frafnar grabbed him by the shirt and pushed him against the wall. "Quiet. I... I need a moment."

Frafnar lowered his head and closed his eyes. Sweat moistened the skin on his forehead. Aden could feel Frafnar trembling. Something was definitely wrong. He sensed the emotions the man struggled with; uncertain what to do, Aden surprised himself. He led with a quick mediocre push with both palms and put all his power into a left hook, connecting with the man's jaw.

Taken off guard, Frafnar was tossed to the side, managing to catch the wall to keep from falling. "I saved your life and this is the thanks I get?"

Frafnar's glare made Aden a little anxious, but he lunged again without explanation. This time Frafnar was ready for it and responded in kind, sending Aden into nearby furnishings. He was quick to defend himself when he landed, fending off Frafnar's assault.

The man was half-orc, giving him an advantage in strength and speed. Aden was trained well, however, and held his own. He dodged and absorbed what he could, and dished out all the energy he could muster. In a brawl like this, he was grateful Frafnar wasn't full orc, or it could have gotten ugly for him. Neither man released a spell, content with an old-fashioned fistfight. They fought until they both slumped to the floor gasping for air, exhausted.

"Now we are even." Aden wiped the blood from his lip.

"What?"

"Back in the wilds, you attacked me when I was losing my head. We're even."

Frafnar glanced sidelong at him then started to chuckle, which blossomed into laughter. Aden smiled and couldn't help but join in.

11

BEHIND THE MASK

"It's like looking in a mirror."

The goblin stared into the orb and found it mesmerizing. The way the reds swirled throughout the blackness of its depths seemed like a mystery he could never truly grasp. He studied it further until he heard the sharp clack of heeled boots approaching. Reluctantly, he tore away his fixation from the artifact as the cloaked figure entered the room. Her long, slender legs quickly shortened the distance to the dais, and she took a seat on her self-proclaimed throne. The goblin had to restrain himself from grabbing at the orb as it escaped his hands and flew toward the woman. The artifact rested gently in her palm and she examined it.

"Do you know what this is? It was a mere rumor, but now

with this, we can move forward immediately. But first, a demonstration."

She snapped her fingers, and a man was dragged into the room by two guards. "Mistress, what have I done to displease you? I swear I'll atone for whatever it was!"

The woman only smirked. "Nothing, but now you'll serve a greater purpose."

The goblin stalked forward with his dagger drawn. The man eyed the weapon in terror and whirled back to his leader, pleading. "Please...no...*no!*"

The dying man collapsed to the ground as the goblin stepped away. The Mistress held the artifact before her and concentrated. The red of the orb glowed and swirled, as if a storm raged within. What had been a corpse moments before rose with lightning reflexes and broke the neck of a guard nearby. Before the second guard could react, the dead man had grabbed the knife from his victim's belt and plunged it into the guard's chest. It didn't take long for the new corpses to rise and stand with the first, silently awaiting their master's commands.

"Excellent!" The Mistress rubbed her hands together, then bellowed commands, "Spread the word, we attack this day! Hit them with everything, and let the fallen fill my ranks!" As the goblin was about to exit the room, the woman's next words made him pause. "Be cautious of guardians," her voice was thick with amusement. "Remember the agony when I treated your last wound. You may not survive that again."

The goblin continued walking and clenched his ghostly hand into a fist. The pain of losing the limb was nothing compared to the agony he'd endured to regain its function. He was unsure how the Mistress had pulled it from his soul, but resolved to never suffer that horror again. He'd been useful to her in the past, but now in light of her newfound power, he was expendable. The goblin expected betrayal; the only question was *when*. As always, he'd be ready.

Weapons clashed as the figures around Aden were locked in deadly battle. Both sides had taken heavy losses, and the fallen bodies littered the ground. The clang of metal against metal filled the air. Weapons piercing armor and slicing flesh. The cries of pain were overwhelming, as was the smell of death. Aden stood amid the chaos but was not part of it. No one attacked him; no one saw him.

Frafnar was only a few paces away, kneeling for a short respite after taking down a formidable foe. Somehow Aden knew Frafnar and his men were desperate and cut off from any reinforcements. Every fiber of his being wished to join them in their struggle, but he was only an observer and had no power to interfere.

Was this a dream? He recalled stories about people who saw visions in their dreams. Perhaps this was one of them, and if it was, why wasn't he there fighting with them?

Frafnar pulled off his mask. His eyes were filled with anger, but Aden saw something more. He saw a deep sadness.

Aden opened his eyes, bringing the ceiling into focus. He sat up, lifted a knee, and tucked his other leg under him. He rested his chin on his knee while he thought about the dream.

Frafnar emerged from the side room, drying his hair with a cloth. They'd laughed about their scuffle he'd started the day before, but Aden was still a little embarrassed. Frafnar had promised to explain everything the next morning. Aden decided to trust him, for now. Frafnar was a man he barely knew, but they'd been through a lot together in such a short time. Since Ohn'na still believed in him, then he would too. Aden hadn't had a chance to tell her about the demose, but the fact that he was alive was a good sign. If Frafnar had wanted him dead, there's no doubt he would be.

As if the man was able to read his thoughts, Frafnar smirked. "I guess you're waiting for that explanation." He flung the cloth on the back of a cushioned chair and sat in it. He clasped his hands behind his head and leaned back, eyes focused on the ceiling. "All right. I assume Ohn'na told you of our mentor, and how Raismus lost his son?"

With a nod from Aden he continued. "When he returned without Garret, even I could see the change in him. You probably heard that my request to become a knight was publicly denied. In reality, it was postponed by the Order to give me the perfect cover, and motive, for my mission. I was to follow Raismus and inform the keepers of his plans. During this time, our mentor came into contact with another group who also schemed to eliminate the Order. However, Raismus wouldn't wait for war, and planned to have the Council disposed of immediately."

Frafnar closed his eyes as if picturing the memories. "When Raismus fell, I continued to wedge my way into the ranks of the other renegades. They have grown more organized in the past few years, and the increased attacks against the Order is from their influence. They intend to create turmoil among the Avant Guard and gain more followers. Trainees are more easily swayed by the demose through the death of their mentors, and the unexplained disappearances of others put the rest on edge."

Aden's hands clenched. He'd felt the effects of their impact firsthand. So this was probably the group that had hired the mercenary to kill Cormell. Aware of the emotions that were building in him, he slowed his breathing and relaxed his hands. This was exactly what they were striving for.

"I've been waiting for their leader to emerge," Frafnar continued, "but the Mistress is careful. I believe she'll show up soon, maybe after the current assignment they've planned. When she does, I'll destroy her."

"You aren't worried they might hear this?" Aden lowered his voice as if all the renegades would swoop down on them at any moment.

"Do you really think I would have lasted this long if I were sloppy?"

"Where are we then?"

"Their forces are spread into smaller camps just inside the borders of the wilds, and that is where we are. Supplies are sent from a secret location, kept even from the captains. I'm certain that's where the leader waits. I haven't been able to uncover much of late, but…" Frafnar paused. It was a minute or two before he spoke again. "You can't stay here."

The statement caught Aden off guard, and he struggled to find words as the man stood. Frafnar suddenly seemed in a rush, dressing and throwing clothes at Aden. Aden held up the garments. "These aren't my clothes—"

"Wear them. They'll identify you as a renegade." Frafnar handed him another object. "This too."

Aden took the mask. "Don't you need this?"

"The renegades haven't seen me without it. I'll be fine. Hurry, I'll escort you to a corves and you can return the mask before you fly to safety."

"You want me to be safe?"

Frafnar didn't respond, only turned away and went into the next room.

Aden studied the mask for a moment. It was smooth like glass, but he knew it was as strong as steel. It was all black except for the deep red where the eyes should be visible, as well as the other faint markings. He sensed unusual magic within it, much like their enchanted blades, and it was much lighter than he'd expected. There must have been a story behind how the man had obtained it, and Aden made a mental note to ask about it one day.

When he brought the mask close to his face, the material flexed and molded to a perfect fit. At first he panicked, as part of it slid behind his head, but then he realized it was to hold it in place. He only thought about removing it, and the material receded to allow him to do so. The mask didn't hinder his vision or breathing in the slightest. Despite its black appearance, he could see through it as if it were transparent. The only indication he was wearing it were the changing deep red runes at the corner of his vision.

He felt strangely empowered by the transformation and imagined that he looked as intimidating as when he'd first seen Frafnar in the wilds. The mask enveloped him in some type of illusion. The deception was so complete that when he tried out a few words, his voice was the same as Frafnar's when he'd worn it. Aden covered his head with the cowl of his cloak and was sliding his gloves on when the man returned.

Frafnar stared at the mask he'd worn for so long. "It's like looking in a mirror." He spoke more to himself than to Aden, but then remembering himself, added, "Use my identity to escape. No one will question you."

With the mask on, Aden felt a little out of his own skin. He needed to ask, "Why are you doing this?" The man was risking a lot to let him escape.

Before Frafnar could respond, an alarm sounded. The smooth aphix stone on a side table glowed brightly and a voice boomed from it, without requiring contact. "All captains will receive their instructions and all units are ordered to report in. The assault shall begin. I repeat—" The voice continued to bellow, but fell on deaf ears as the two men viewed the target on the wall, displayed by the stone.

"One of the newly established outposts, Orian Citadel..." Aden turned to Frafnar and waited for a reaction. When there was none, Aden protested. "You can't actually be considering this."

Frafnar's face revealed nothing. "I'm going to need that mask back after all." His voice was devoid of any emotion.

"Didn't you hear?" Aden shouted. "They're going to attack a citadel! People are going to die. Our friends! How can you—?"

"Their leader will show herself after this mission, I'm certain of it. This is the only chance I'll get, and if I'm not present it will look suspicious. I must go. She's testing everyone. Most of the casualties will happen in the first assault; she will corrupt those she captures. I will try to minimize the losses as best I can." Frafnar reached for the mask.

Aden turned and shook his head in disbelief. He couldn't let this happen; even if Frafnar did all he could, lives would be lost.

"If the leader isn't dealt with," Frafnar continued, taking a step toward Aden, "more people will die."

The tension between them was growing but before either could act, there was a loud knock and the door opened. A darkly clad renegade in full armor and helmet entered the room. "Captain Armastus, here are your battle plans. I've been ordered to accompany you to your corves." The renegade handed Aden the sealed parchment.

Aden backed away from the man next to him. "We will continue this later."

Frafnar's jaw clenched but otherwise he remained still. Aden followed the renegade to the doorway but glanced back at Frafnar before he went through. The discussion was over.

As Aden marched through the corridor after the renegade. Aden did his best to appear confident, as Frafnar would have.

When he met up with Frafnar's unit, and they acknowledged him as their captain, he was more at ease. Soon all were in the air on beasts they called corves. However, when they arrived at their destination, Aden almost lost his composure at the scene he witnessed. Orian Citadel was already burning.

12

A DARK DAY

"Don't go!"

Smoke lay thick in the air, and rubble littered the area. Orian Citadel was almost unrecognizable after the outer defenses had been breached. The inner halls were in no better shape, with toppled statues, mounds of debris, scorched areas from errant spells, and the metallic smell of blood in the air. Fighting could be heard in the distance, while explosions rained outside. A large group of knights were trying to give others time to escape by drawing the main enemy forces away. The knights hadn't been beaten, not yet.

The battle plans revealed that Frafnar's unit was responsible for infiltrating the heart of the citadel and dealing with any formidable resistance. Aden hadn't visited this citadel before, and its ravaged halls were unknown to him. He averted his eyes from the bodies that lay on the ground, both renegade and Avant Guard alike. A part of him desperately wanted to memorize each face he'd been too late to save, but the fear that he'd recognize someone kept his gaze away. He couldn't bear to think of it.

To his relief, they hadn't met any resistance while they scoured the corridors toward the center. If they met anyone from the Order, he knew there would be battle. Realizing his options were limited, Aden decided to separate himself from Frafnar's men. An opportunity presented itself when they came upon a corridor that was heavily guarded by explosive runes. The magic was strategically planted, leaving no possible way they could pass without setting it off. Even with magic of their own, it was likely the traps would cause the ceiling to fall.

Aden smiled behind the mask. He could order the men to follow him. While he could make it, most of them would be lost to... Aden shook off the dark thought. No. He wouldn't abuse his position to hurt anyone if it could be avoided. "Find a way around. I'm going on ahead."

Before any protests for his safety began, Aden used a spell to quicken his movements and ran toward the obvious trap. He suspected the damage would be considerable, enough to alert his people to the approaching danger and block the passage.

Aden felt the explosions shift the air as he barely stayed ahead of the blasts. The floor trembled beneath his feet and debris rained over his head. He remembered how Frafnar had used the same method to escape from their draquor pursuers. Adrenaline fueled him forward like it had back then, but this time he was prepared for what must be done.

As the last of the rubble settled into place, Aden stood and dusted himself off and listened. Confident his plan had worked and Frafnar's unit searched for an alternate route, Aden continued until he heard fighting ahead. He removed the mask and shoved it inside his jerkin. When he entered the next chamber, Knight Freesha was the first person he recognized in the chaos of combat. The room her group battled in was large, with rows of columns supporting the ceiling. Aden joined in the skirmish and helped dispatch several of the renegades until no threats remained.

The group was clearly on edge and alert to any enemy reinforcements, so Aden called out to them before he approached. "Knight Freesha! What are you doing here? Where's Khodi?"

The elderly woman paused to speak with him but motioned for her group to keep going. "Aden Fendrie, I could ask you the same question." Her grip tightened around the verge stone she held. "Khodi mentioned she had spoken to you. Our assignment was to help manage the concerns of this emerging outpost. We were attacked without warning—the defenses of the citadel were unprepared for an assault of such magnitude." The knight glanced around like she expected someone to show up at any moment. "Khodi was here, but we were separated..." Freesha shook the unresponsive verge stone. "Come on, girl, answer."

Aden hid his grin as he imagined Khodi stomping on the rock in a comical way. He could almost hear her words: "Damn you, old bat, I'm coming!" He was about to explain, but he heard the clamor of more enemies advancing. "You have to go. I'll block the passage from here if you can do the same on the other side."

The woman agreed, and Aden waited until she was far enough down the passage. Together they used their combined power to make the walls and ceiling shake and crack, then finally begin to fall. The knight's verge stone came alive with light, and Freesha yelled over the noise as the stone structure collapsed between them. "Khodi's in trouble! Aden, find her!"

The passage was blocked before Aden could respond, and sweat beaded his brow from the effort of the magic. He managed to don the mask an instant before the renegades rejoined him.

"Captain! Are you all right?" one of the men asked him, while most of Frafnar's unit were enthralled by the extensive cave-in.

Aden did his best to portray an authoritative image. He nodded and imagined what Frafnar would say. "They are escaping! Find them!"

All the men straightened to attention. "Yes, sir!"

As they pushed on to find an adjoining corridor, Aden used the opportunity to slip away. He had to find Khodi, and quickly. After turning a corner, Aden felt a rapid succession of taps on his head. He looked up to find Freesha's small bird fluttering there. Since the pet hadn't been with the knight, Aden suspected it could help him. "Do you know where Khodi is? Take me to her!"

The bird was already flying away and then back to him, as if urging him to follow. He couldn't fathom how the creature had recognized him through his disguise, but he hurried after it. He trailed the thing halfway across the citadel before they finally came to a small courtyard. Any renegades he crossed paths with hurried by without a hint of suspicion. The mask identified him as Captain Armastus, who was not to be questioned.

The glass that had covered the area was shattered and no longer kept the rain out. The water fell lightly, but steadily, having already drenched the plants and the charred earth. Aden pictured several scenarios of enemies overcoming Khodi as he continued to follow the bird through the foliage. He froze when a familiar voice spoke to him, originating from behind a broken column.

"So, you've come to finish the job. Well, you'd better hurry... or you might miss your chance."

Aden was relieved to hear Khodi's voice. She faced away from him, and sat on the ground with her back against the pillar. Once he drew nearer to her, the shock made him drop to a knee. His friend was before him, her hands at a wound to her midsection.

"Well?" Khodi's eyes remained defiant, ready, and unwavering.

Aden noticed a hint of something else as well. It was pity, for the one who Khodi thought was here to kill her. He took off the mask and tossed it to the side. "I'm not one of them."

Khodi's eyes widened. "Aden! What are you doing here? You have to—" When she tried to stand her face wrenched with pain and she slumped back.

The paryl pick was held in her bloodied hand. He knew that the small needle was coated with a potent plant, an anesthetic that would spread through the bloodstream and numb her body. It was one of the standard items members of the Order carried with them. Without it, the pain from severe wounds would be unbearable.

Aden roused all his power and focused on a healing spell, but the damage was considerable and she'd already lost so much blood. Khodi had done as much as she could, but it was far from enough. None of it would be enough. They needed a master healer. Given the sounds of battle still raging, Aden doubted that any were nearby. "Hold on, just hold on. I'm going to get you out of here."

She didn't seem to be listening. Khodi's head was tilted back, and her eyes searched the clouds above while rainwater slid down her face. "Why does it always rain... at times like this? I would've liked to see the sun." Her eyes lowered to Aden. "At least I got to see you again... one last time."

"Don't talk like that." It was hard for Aden to hide the panic in his voice. "We are going to get you help. We are going to—" His tears fell and mingled with the rain, but the calm of her voice made him listen.

"Aden. I... don't have much time. I can feel it. Please... I have something important to tell you. I managed to defeat one of their captains." Khodi took in a deep breath and let it out slowly. "I had taken care of his guards first, and was sure after he'd fallen I was alone. But... I was struck from behind. I didn't see who it was, but... it must be important."

"I swear I'll find the one who did this." Aden's voice trembled.

"No." Khodi raised a hand and wiped some of the moisture

from his face. "Promise me you won't surrender to the demose. Not someone as... noble as... you. Aden..."

"I promise!"

She gave him a small weak smile and Aden watched in denial as the life faded from her eyes. He hugged her. "Khodi..." *Don't go...* "Khodi." *Freesha is worried about you...* "Khodi!" *We need to see that sun.* "Someone help me!" *Don't go!*

Ohn'na saw the smoke rising from the burning citadel in the distance. She had been drawn here by an undeniable compulsion. The Council had allowed only a handful of knights to accompany her to scout it out. They kept out of sight, picking up those who made it to safety beyond the grounds of the citadel. They didn't have the numbers for an assault, but help was coming. She feared it would be too late, though.

Ohn'na bent over and gasped sharply, her hand clutching at her chest. It felt like an electrical charge pulsed through her body. She knew it was because of Aden. His power was growing indeed if others could be affected by his strong outbursts of pain.

A nearby knight noticed and went to her side. "Guardian Sazi, are you all right?"

She waved the man off. "Yes, yes. Let's concentrate on getting the survivors out."

"Yes, ma'am!"

Ohn'na squared her shoulders and made up her mind. She

headed to the already tired—but patiently waiting —wyvernkin.

Aden opened his eyes and saw a pair of boots, and a familiar voice spoke with a distinct sincerity.

"I'm sorry." Frafnar bowed respectfully before the dead girl. He picked up his mask, and after he'd spat on the severed head of Captain Zeffron, returned it to its rightful place.

With one hand, Aden closed Khodi's eyes and clenched her sword tightly with his other. He was torn. The emotions raged within him, but Khodi's words kept him from toppling over the edge of his senses. Aden swore he wouldn't disappoint her; he wouldn't betray her trust.

As he stood, a man entered the courtyard at a frantic run. A group of renegades chased the clearly terrified man, but Frafnar ordered them to hold their positions. He was a simple laborer and no threat to them. Aden and Frafnar shared a look, which was abruptly broken as a knife spun through the air between them. The blade struck the fleeing man in the back and he fell, never to rise again. Everyone stared at the body until a voice shifted their attention to the hall where the laborer had come from.

"That one almost got away. Couldn't have that, could we, Captain?"

Hearing these words, Aden's heart raced and his throat tightened. Horrible visions of Cormell's death flashed in his mind as the same creature from his nightmares stepped into the rain from the corridor. Aden's focus shifted between the goblin's ghostly hand and his red eyes beneath the wide-brimmed hat. It was him; it *had* to be him. He could never forget that voice or deadly glare, and the spectral limb was too unusual to be a coincidence. Had the goblin murdered Khodi? The thought only intensified his rage. As Khodi asked, he wouldn't rely on the demose, but he would seek retribution for those he'd lost, and for all the others who had suffered.

Another large group of screaming workers hurried down the hall behind the creature and wisely avoided the courtyard. The goblin peered over his shoulder, then returned to face the masked captain once again. "Gather your men, there is more sport to be had!" And with that the creature turned to hunt more prey.

"Don't." Frafnar warned Aden. "He'll kill you."

Aden ignored him and dashed after the creature.

"Stop him. We need him alive!" Aden heard Frafnar call to the renegades.

There were sounds of pursuit, but Aden wouldn't be deterred, not when Cormell's killer was within his reach. He'd found him! By some miracle he'd found him. He wouldn't let this chance slip away. He would not.

13

CHASING SHADOWS

"You killed Guardian Cormell."

Aden raced past broken pillars and chunks of debris. Fires raged, scarring stone and leaving the air filled with smoke. A lump constricted Aden's throat and his eyes stung. There was a heavy weight in his chest; the loss he'd endured was still raw and painful. His legs carried him, but his will drove him. At times he would lose sight of the goblin he chased, only to glimpse the creature rounding the next corner. He ran wildly, but he soon lost track of the goblin completely.

He could no longer hear the explosions of battle, and he found the ensuing silence eerie and oppressive. He crouched behind some rubble to catch his breath. The corridor was dark and empty. His eyes searched warily, while his imagination played out a scenario in which the creature had doubled back for the kill. He was being followed, of that he was certain. He'd escaped Frafnar's men in his impulsive chase, but it had yet to be seen whether they were the ones who now dogged him, or whether this was the emergence of a new threat. He listened carefully. It wasn't any sound that alerted him but a strong gut feeling. An impulse to move on. Moments later, a figure appeared in the same place he'd been and continued in pursuit.

Leave me alone! Aden thought, as sweat dampened his hair and cooled his skin. It wasn't long before his pursuers began trying to herd him. Clearly, they didn't intend to kill him, but forced him in a different direction by wild swings with their blades.

After a time, Aden knew he'd been cornered. He stood with his back to the wall, unable to escape. He gripped Khodi's tarnished sword tightly, the blade held before him. The men following him held back, giving him a wide berth, and watched him while they awaited further orders.

It wasn't long before Frafnar stood among them. "There's nowhere left to run. Surrender and come with me."

Aden's only response was an unyielding stare.

"Go," Frafnar commanded his men.

The warriors stalked forward and formed a semicircle around their prey. Aden closed his eyes, taking in the moment. He felt his heart pounding in his aching chest, and he focused on that predictable rhythm. He opened his eyes, and the first attacker took his swing. Aden deflected it easily, but from then on, the movements became a blur. The attacks were swift and precise as the men worked as a team to find a break in Aden's defenses. He was hard-pressed to keep them all at bay. The battle reminded Aden of a dance, increasing in rhythm, faster and faster, until abruptly, it ended.

Aden froze as a dark blade stopped inches from his face. His weapon clanged against another while numerous more paused barely inches from his body. He couldn't move without injury, so he remained rooted in place with only his chest heaving from the exertion.

There was a sound of slow clapping, and the goblin stepped from the shadows with a smirk on his lips. "Bravo. That was quite the show." His attention was drawn to Aden's sharp glare. "And from where do I know you...?"

Aden dared not retaliate against the blades around him; his voice remained low but thick with contempt. "You killed Guardian Cormell."

The creature tilted his head in thought at the title, and he touched his spectral hand as if reliving the agony. "Guardian..."

"The very same who severed your limb." Aden raised his chin proudly, yet his heart ached from the memory. Guilt stabbed him, twisting his insides. He was certain that Cormell could have defeated the creature if he hadn't been there, if he hadn't been a burden. Aden buried the regret and refocused his energies on Cormell's killer.

The goblin's gaze shot back to Aden and his hands balled into fists. "I see. Fitting that you joined our ranks—but you tried to attack an agent of the Mistress. You certainly cannot be allowed to live."

A loud horn sounded, the signal to return. Drawing a knife, the creature stepped forward, but Frafnar blocked his path.

"We are to retreat. We'd best not leave the Mistress waiting."

"Just kill him and be done with it." The creature huffed and threw the knife with such skill that anyone who hadn't been watching closely would have missed it.

The blade had already passed Frafnar before he recognized the danger. As he turned, he heard the sickening thump of metal embed into flesh. The knife had found a mark. Khodi stood there, only a few inches in front of Aden. The blank stare of the dead girl was chilling. It was even more unnerving when she looked down at the knife that protruded from her chest and yanked it out without complaint.

With the blade in hand, she pointed the weapon at the goblin. "You will return to the Mistress without further delay." Her tone was even, but the threat was plain.

The creature glared at her but turned on his heels and strode away. Khodi then retrieved her sword from Aden's limp grasp and replaced it at her hip. She said no more and waited nearby like a silent guard.

Reality hit Frafnar like a flash of lightning. So this was what the Mistress had planned. To obtain the device and supply her army from the dead of her enemy. Frafnar clenched his teeth. Why hadn't he seen this coming? "Bring the prisoner," he ordered.

Frafnar watched his men lead Aden away, who appeared

so stunned he barely took notice. Aden's voice was so low when he spoke that Frafnar almost missed it.

"Khodi?"

Ohn'na knew she was in the right place when she sensed Aden nearby. She'd commandeered one of the corves near the crippled citadel and had easily followed the others. The camp had been easier to infiltrate than she had expected, as the renegades seemed more preoccupied with preparations than with checking each rider that flew in. She was one of the last to arrive, and even as her feet touched the ground she could tell they were preparing to deploy elsewhere. Pondering this development, Ohn'na darted through a door to a building nearby. Fortunately, some cloaks had been left in the changing chamber, and she wasted no time donning one and lifted the hood to hide her face. Hopefully this would allow her to blend in and walk around more freely.

Aden was alive; she knew it. She needed to find the trainee and bide her time until she could free him. Ohn'na tightened the cloak around her and hurried onward.

Somewhere nearby, Aden hugged his knees and looked through the magical containment field that separated him and the girl who had been his friend. Other prisoners—mostly trainees—were also detained in the same area, but Aden barely registered their presence.

Khodi was alive. But from what he'd seen, he knew that alive was not the right word. No matter how much he pleaded with her, she only stood there with that vacuous stare while guarding the captives. He couldn't bear to see her this way.

Aden rested his head on his knees. Why had Frafnar brought him here? Where was he? He closed his eyes and waited for whatever was to come.

Frafnar couldn't help but feel smug at the scowls the other captains gave him. He'd been the first to be aware of Zeffron's death and immediately seized his squad. The others had missed the chance, and Frafnar knew the additional warriors would prove useful if he played them correctly. His disposition shifted to a more serious mood as he evaluated the situation. The renegades had conjured portals and were escaping to long-abandoned ruins in the wilds. *So this is where you've been hiding.*

Their leader stood before the assembly, on worn steps that had once led up to an old forgotten citadel. Her devout agents were strategically positioned on the lower steps before her like a wall of protection, and Frafnar counted the goblin as one of them. At the base of the stairs, the captains stood before their men, who were in organized rows. The undead rigidly waited in their own formations on the outer parts of the assembly. This made Frafnar nervous, especially those who flanked each captain. His only consolation was knowing that his own men were nearby.

The prisoners who had been collected during the retreat were penned within a circle of the undead guards. Frafnar spotted Aden, who seemed uninjured and secure for the moment. Capturing him had been the only way to ensure his safety, but Frafnar had no intention of letting any harm come to him or to the other prisoners. The leader was before him now, and it was only a matter of time until she would be dealt with. As if reading his thoughts, her voice grabbed his attention.

"The first assault on the Order has been a success, and we've gained more than we could have hoped for! Through your efforts, we can accelerate our plans and move forward. But first, there is a matter that must be addressed. There's a pretender among you!"

Frafnar tensed slightly, thankful for the emanating aura of the mask, but then realized she wasn't looking at him. Was there also another working against the Mistress that he was unaware of? Had the Order sent someone to aid him, or was it one of her lackeys hoping to usurp her? The renegade leader erased all of his inquiries with her next words.

"You have come, sooner than I expected. Impressive. But no matter, you are here now. Isn't that right, Ohn'na Sazi?"

Well, isn't she full of surprises? Frafnar thought.

Several undead surrounded a cloaked figure standing near the hostages with the cowl pulled low over its face. Since she no longer had anything to gain from remaining disguised,

Ohn'na pushed back her hood. "You seem to know me, but I don't know you."

The leader's voice was low and sounded callous. "I would never forget your presence, even with your feeble attempts to hide it. You know me, and by the end, you will remember."

"Ohn'na!"

The guardian turned in Aden's direction. "It will be okay."

The leader smirked and produced a scroll from her robes. "Ah yes, my spies informed me that you had finally taken on a pupil. It's fortunate he's here." She removed the magical field then pointed to one of the undead guards. "Take him."

Frafnar tried to push forward, but the undead that flanked him blocked his way and pressed in closer.

The dead-eyed guard grabbed Aden and held him securely. Aden felt the blade at his neck. It was Khodi who readied it for the strike.

"Kill him," the leader commanded.

Aden's eyes widened, and the word slipped from his lips. "Khodi?"

The tears he'd shed were still wet on his face, falling on the hand that held a fistful of his clothing. The blade moved to strike but stopped short only inches from its mark, and remained there.

"Kill him!" the leader yelled louder. She threw the scroll to the side and took out an orb from her robes.

Aden felt Khodi's body shaking, struggling between striking him and letting him go. "Come on, Khodi, fight it!"

"Kill them all!" the leader screamed and retreated up the stairs and out of sight.

In the next few seconds, those who were closest to the undead were the first to be cut down, and rose to join those who'd killed them. The captains were among them, faces riddled with shock at the treachery of their leader. Frafnar was an exception. Thanks to his squad he was spared, and only a few of the men behind him were taken. "She has betrayed us!" he yelled. "Fight! *Fight!*"

It was apparent that the Mistress would rather control her force as corpses—no one could betray her that way—but she was unaware of the limits to the artifact: command too many and you lose control.

Khodi's blade pulled back from Aden's neck and her vacant eyes centered to where the renegade leader had disappeared. She started off in that direction, cutting down any other undead in her way, and pursued the woman.

Ohn'na also managed to force the undead away. She untied and protected the prisoners. "Glad to see you are still in one piece," she said as she delivered Aden's weapon.

Aden gestured in agreement as he searched for and caught a glimpse of his friend. He was alive because of her, because she was resisting the controlling magic. It was strange to see her fighting again after witnessing her death, but Aden dared to hope that she might still be saved.

He deflected a sweeping strike against him, and a retaliation of his own caused his attacker to disintegrate into dust when Aden's sword sliced through it. He was about to follow in Khodi's footsteps when he spotted the goblin cutting down his own assailants amid the fighting. He didn't care about the creature's predicament, but he did notice he was working his way out of the throng of violent corpses. He was trying to escape, but Aden refused to allow that. He heard Ohn'na call out to him as he plunged into the chaos. He knew she wanted to chase after him, but her duty to defend the captives would be her priority. She would have to trust that he knew what he was doing.

14

———

LAST FAREWELL

"Free."

Aden darted toward the goblin, weaving his way through the battle between the living and the undead. He cut down any corpses that blocked his way or took a swipe at him. In light of the betrayal, the renegades put their differences aside and fought alongside the guardian and the captives. Frafnar was yelling orders, keeping the survivors in some type of controlled chaos. They defended themselves well under his command, and Aden couldn't help but wonder how the renegades would feel once they realized the deception of their captain. The odds were against them, and if they survived, they'd be wise to flee or surrender.

The battle became a blur to Aden, but as he neared his quarry the goblin saw him coming. The creature sneered at him as he broke through the swarm of battling forces. When Aden made it through as well, he spotted the goblin fleeing toward the trees. He followed without hesitation, leaving the sound of fighting behind. He remained in pursuit until the creature disappeared through a group of conifers. Aden hurried after him, cutting his way through the dense branches. When he reached the other side, the world was shrouded in darkness. There was nothing in the endless black, except for a sword embedded in the ground. The weapon was basked in a pale light that shone from the sky. It was Cormell's blade.

Aden heard the goblin's words echo around him, making it difficult to pinpoint the origin. "The guardian couldn't defeat me, and yet you still pursue me. What hope could *you* possibly have?"

"I'm not the one hiding," Aden responded, continuing to search the area while his eyes adjusted to the dark. This was an illusion, the goblin's magic seeming almost tangible. It was an obvious trap for such a clever creature. He was using Cormell's blade to lure him in, like a moth to the flame.

"You should have died that day."

"And yet, here I am." Aden carefully edged forward, toward the weapon, despite his awareness of the ruse.

"The guardian sacrificed his life for nothing. In the end, you will die."

"I'm not dead yet."

The goblin was nowhere to be seen, but Aden felt his scrutiny. After several paces, the ground beneath Aden's feet flashed a green light, but he had a transpo spell ready before the rune magic could ensnare him. *Not this time.* It was the same trap he'd fallen prey to before, and he refused to be taken in by it again.

The rune remained visible, and dozens like it appeared and glowed around the area. They began to rotate and orbit the blade in the center at varying speeds and distances. Aden had little trouble navigating the maze of traps and closed the distance to Cormell's weapon. He warily entered the pale light while feeling unnervingly exposed. Aden reached out to touch the blade, wondering if the creature would taunt him with the real sword. Relief surged through him as his fingertips touched the hilt. It was real.

Aden only had an instant with Cormell's blade before the goblin hurled himself through the air with daggers leading the attack. He blasted his assailant with a force of magic that repelled the assault, but the creature was quick to return with even more vigor. The goblin lunged at him with savage strikes. Aden bore his sword and leaped away while parrying the attacks. He kept the momentum and sped up his movements to allow some distance between himself and his adversary. However, the goblin wouldn't be denied and sent knife after knife spinning through the air after him. Aden ran in a circle, parallel with one of the green runes, careful to dodge and deflect the blades; the weapons were undoubtedly poisoned.

The creature had yet another trick up his sleeve, and used his powers to conjure several duplicate copies of himself. He commanded them to attack Aden while he slipped away into the shadows. The knives that flew at Aden increased tenfold, and he was unable to avoid them all. The grazing wounds were painful, but adrenaline fueled him, and he ignored them. He took comfort in knowing that conjured blades couldn't be poisoned. One of the clones blocked his way to disrupt his momentum, but Aden took two large steps and used the clone's shoulders as an anchor as his feet flew overhead. Another adversary appeared before him, and he sank the end of his blade deep into the clone before spinning away as it vaporized in a puff of smoke.

Aden was doing well to avoid the dangers and was trying to concoct a plan to draw out the goblin when he was blasted off his feet. He saw the group of duplicates who combined their powers to hurl him through the air. His breath caught in his throat as he crossed the threshold to one of the green runes. He scrambled up, but the magic ensnared and paralyzed him. He saw the eel creatures floating at the edge of his vision and felt the sharp pain of their fangs. The goblin stepped out of the shadows, while Aden's cry of agony rang out as a tendril of electricity stabbed him.

"It was your fault, you know, that your guardian was killed."

Aden held back any more expressions of pain, refusing to offer further amusement for the creature. He focused his attention solely on the goblin.

"Now." The creature held up his spectral hand, which green fire had engulfed once again. "Let's end this the way it was meant to."

Aden's laughter made the goblin pause. "Don't you think I spent every single day working out how I could have escaped this trap and helped my guardian?"

The creature swept his arm forward, but Aden's body

gleamed with brilliance, and tendrils of his own electricity crackled and sparked. Now able to move, Aden fell to a knee and expelled the magic. A blast of electricity burst from him, while finer lines cut through the air. The clones and eels vanished as the current hit them, and the green of the runes changed to a bright blue as the added energy charged the magic. Blown back by the force, the goblin was now caught in one of his own overcharged runes. The creature cried out in agony before there was a flash of light and a sound like breaking glass. The goblin had freed himself and crumpled to the ground as steam rose from his body. Weakened, he pulled himself up on his knees and stared at the tip of Aden's sword that hovered a few inches from his face. Aden towered over his enemy, and an inner conflict raged within. It was his duty to arrest the creature for trial, but his feelings demanded that he enact his own justice.

The goblin scoffed at him. "Your hesitation reeks of weakness. Your Order is feeble because they hold fast to compassion. The wise do not hesitate, and the strong do not show mercy. Do you think we showed any such things when we sacked your citadel and killed your friends?"

Aden's anger flared as he pictured the creature ambushing Khodi. He raised his sword for a final blow when he felt something stop him, as if a hand had grabbed his wrist. Nothing could deter him now, but then the memory of Cormell's words resonated. *Revenge isn't our way.*

Aden blinked and the feeling left him, and his weapon remained poised to strike. Nothing held him back now. It was his decision—to betray or follow the ideals of the Order. He lowered his blade slowly as clarity subdued the anger. "You couldn't have killed her; it was the undead she wasn't aware of." Aden made a motion with his hand and summoned a rope that slithered around the goblin to secure him in place. "You will be judged for your crimes, as is our way." Aden turned and was reaching to retrieve Cormell's sword when the creature's words made him pause.

"I will not be humiliated like this!" The goblin's body then morphed into a creature with a long snout, furry body, sharp teeth, and wicked claws. His transformation broke his bonds and he sprang at Aden. "*Just die!*"

With a calm he hadn't felt before, Aden held his course and pulled Cormell's blade from the ground. On impulse, he pointed it at his assailant, who gaped in shock as his own momentum impaled him on the weapon. Aden removed the tarnished sword from the goblin's chest, who then fell to the ground. The creature's ghostly hand faded, and the look of disbelief remained on his face as his eyes clouded over in death.

The illusory magic dissipated, and the sun shone once again, Aden tilted his head to the sky and closed his eyes. He took in a deep breath. *It's finally over.* He'd found Cormell's sword, and now it was time to put it to rest.

When Aden returned to the ruins, he witnessed the last of the undead fall and the remaining renegades and prisoners directing their weapons at each other. Frafnar stepped in as reinforcements flew overhead on their wyvernkins. "Your leader is beaten, and more Avant Guard will be here soon. Either submit or run. Fighting will get you nowhere. If you surrender, the Order may show mercy."

Some did run, while others threw down their weapons. A few tried to fight but were easily subdued. Aden let them deal with the renegades while he ran to where Khodi and the Mistress had gone. Now able to leave her charges under the care of others, Ohn'na followed him. They arrived to find the renegade leader defeated, and Khodi sitting and staring at the dead woman. Their wounds were a testament to the fierce battle between them, as well as the extensive damage to the area.

"Khodi?"

The girl's head turned slowly and she struggled with the words. "A-Aden. My... friend."

"That's right," Aden replied in relief and reached to her.

Khodi had the artifact in one hand and her sword in the other. She put the hilt of the weapon in Aden's hand and smiled. "Free," she said and sighed.

She lifted the orb and threw it on the ground, shattering it. Her smile was the last thing Aden saw before she disappeared. He couldn't stop the tears that fell now that she was truly gone.

Ohn'na stood nearby. The girl's body disintegrated like all the other undead they had defeated. She examined the dead woman and recognized her to be one of the first members of the Order who went missing. Ohn'na had no connection to this person, so why the vendetta against her? She tried to focus on the matters at hand, but the question still lingered in the back of her mind.

Ohn'na backed away, giving Aden the time alone that he needed. She found Frafnar helping to wrap a wound, and was finishing as Ohn'na approached. Frafnar looked up at her, appearing ready for any judgment she would give.

Ohn'na held out her hand, an offer to help him stand. "It's time to come home. Welcome back."

15

———

KNIGHT FENDRIE

"I will protect."

———————————————————————

Guardian Ohn'na Sazi stood on the top landing of the stairs. Behind her was the door to the main hall of the ruined citadel. She recalled her history, hearing the stories of structures such as this falling to the orcs in wars long past. Such places remained unclaimed, absorbed into the wilds that grew near unexplored or perilous environs. Ohn'na wasn't concerned, though; the renegade leader had been using it for some time, so the area had probably been left alone.

She brought her focus back to the two young men before her. She cradled her sword in her arm, the tip of the blade near her shoulder and the hilt in her palm. She raised her voice so the dozen or so witnesses heard her every word. "We have suffered more than anyone could have thought possible in the past few days. But if it wasn't for the bravery, ingenuity, and determination of these two trainees, more lives would have been lost."

Ohn'na flipped and spun her weapon so it was now flat against the back of her arm, the point visible from behind her shoulder. The two young men held their downturned swords before them as they knelt, their hands on the hilt of their blades while the points were pressed into the stone below. She took Frafnar's weapon first. In the hilt the violet gem caught the rays of sunlight and shone brilliantly. It dawned on Ohn'na that she hadn't seen him use his dagger since their reunion, and briefly wondered why. It wasn't needed for the ceremony, however.

"Frafnar Armastus." She took his sword and turned it horizontally so the flat of the weapon reflected the sky. "I find you worthy of this blade, for your devotion to your mission, and your amazing strength against the demose." She placed his weapon in his waiting palms.

"I will protect." Frafnar spoke the words of ceremony. He touched his forehead to the cool steel and with one motion he sheathed it while still kneeling, keeping his head bowed.

Ohn'na moved to Aden next, whose pose was the reflection of the man beside him. She took his sword and did the same as before. "Aden Fendrie." She paused as if to consider her choice.

Aden looked up at her. She saw the flash of worry in his eyes, but it all melted away when he saw her face. She was smiling, a gentle, warm, all-encompassing smile. There was no doubt, only certainty.

Ohn'na took his sword. "I find you worthy of this blade, for the lives you have saved, including my own. For rejecting the demose, despite their tempting promises, and for helping a fellow member return home. Most of all, for remembering those we lost. They help shape who we are, and who we will become. The fond memories strengthen us, and we should never forget them." She returned the weapon to him.

"I will protect." Aden said, and Ohn'na heard the whole-hearted conviction in his tone. He tapped the flat of the blade against his forehead, then slid his weapon back into place at his side and remained kneeling.

"I, who have been given the authority by the keepers of Longshield Citadel, hereby proclaim these men worthy of the Avant Guard." Her voice amplified for the dramatic moment. "Rise! Knights of Mythreth!"

16

CEREMONY

"She... would have liked that."

Aden couldn't contain his curiosity. "So, I still don't understand why the Council allowed you to do the ceremony here instead of at the citadel. It's unlike them to change tradition."

"In times of war, such customs weren't so unusual. The situation now isn't as dire as that, but the Order hasn't seen an attack like this for many years. The destruction to Orian Citadel was extensive, and a great number of our people fell. We are being transferred there to help them recover and lend a hand in rebuilding and managing the concerns of the region."

"I see." Aden was delighted, but at the same time a part of him longed to return to the place he'd considered his home for so long. It was a great honor to be chosen to do this, especially since he wasn't a seasoned knight. He then realized something. "We?"

Ohn'na grinned. "You may not be my trainee anymore, but don't think you'll have all the fun without me. And since Frafnar wasn't assigned a post prior to this, he'll be joining us."

Aden had assumed that once this was all over, he'd see little of them "Well, I'm glad. We've been through so much together in such a short time. Saying goodbye now... wouldn't be easy."

"I thought so too. That's why I put in the request to Keeper Nannelle. Which reminds me, she sends her best wishes. She'd tell you herself but her duties called her away, you understand." Ohn'na showed him the aphix stone she carried with her.

"Isn't that heavy?" Aden asked. It was large compared to the customary verge stones that were commonly used by knights in the field. The aphix stone was bigger, but so too was the range over which it could be used.

Ohn'na laughed. "Yes, but the burden was worth it. With this, I was able to report the situation to the keepers. That's how the others knew where to find us."

"It sounds like you're the one who should be getting the praise today." Aden smiled.

"You can't *always* be the hero." Ohn'na matched his grin with one of her own. "Well, I must get back. Before we leave we'll be erecting a pyre to honor those we lost. I will see you there."

As Aden watched her go he caught sight of Freesha leaving

as well. She'd been there as a witness for the ceremony too? Aden called out to her. "Knight Freesha!"

She paused, which allowed him to catch up with her. The sadness in her eyes was so deep he lost his words; her grief mirrored his own. After a few moments she broke the silence. "Congratulations on your official entry into the Order."

"Thank you… actually, there was something I wished to talk to you about."

She waited as he removed the extra scabbard and belt from his waist, and presented it to her. "Khodi would have wanted me to give you this."

Freesha's hands shook slightly. He'd already informed her of Khodi's fate, but to see the weapon confirmed it. She pulled the blade back from the darkness of its sheath, bathing it in sunlight once more. But the weapon had lost its vitality, the same as its master. She couldn't bear to look at it for long and returned it to Aden. "Take it to the gardens of this place, and lay it to rest. She… would have liked that."

Aden struggled with the lump in his throat and the stinging of his eyes as Freesha walked past him. He'd broken down too many times already; he could only imagine becoming a dehydrated prune if he didn't control his emotions. It was the same when he'd lost Cormell. He regained his composure and headed to the gardens, or what was left of them in these ruins. He had a personal ceremony of his own to carry out.

When he found it, he came to discover that the place was wildly overgrown. Where once organized and frequently tended flora embellished the grounds, now unruly weeds flourished. The hardy grass areas had defended their claim well, as few larger plants took root among them. The grass was long, but Aden's polished blade shortened it easily. He sheared a large enough area that he could sit comfortably.

Freesha had been right: Khodi would've liked this place. Despite being unkempt and abandoned, it was peaceful. Aden took his friend's sword from its scabbard and drove the end into the ground. He sat back to examine it. The once unblemished steel had darkened to a bleak and hazy silver, no longer reflecting the light in brilliance. The gem too had become clouded, the spark of life gone. The edge, which was always razor sharp, had dulled, as if the weapon had yielded and died with its master—the magic within had dissipated, so in a sense it had.

He took another weapon from his belt and secured it into the ground next to Khodi's. Cormell's sword, a shadow of its former splendor like the companion blade beside it. Once a member of the Order died, it was customary to return their weapon to the fires in which it was forged. Somehow, though, Aden found it more fitting that the weapons remained here. A place of peace—the very thing that they'd fought and died for. It might take centuries, but the blades would eventually rejoin the fires. For now, it felt right to give them some time in the sun, surrounded by the flowers, trees, and grasses. The calm would be a suitable retirement for the weapons, until the day they returned to their source.

Aden closed his eyes, took a deep breath and let it out slowly. He wouldn't make the same mistake he had with Cormell. If Khodi's spirit remained in this world, he would see that she had closure. He followed the same method as before, calming his mind and reaching out with it. His senses became more acute, distinctly feeling the soft breeze in his hair and the warmth of the sun on his skin. He inhaled the mixed fragrance of earth, grass, and flowers, and heard the wind sweep through the trees. The buzzing of nearby insects and the chirping of birds completed the serenity of the gardens.

After some time, he opened his eyes. He sensed nothing; she was gone. Khodi had moved on; nothing compelled her to remain in this world. He thought about it for a while, and he realized that everything had been said. She'd had faith in him to be strong, and so he would be. He missed her, but she was at peace.

His gaze returned to the weapons standing before him. He slid his sword from his side and sank it into the ground beside them. The differences were remarkable, as the pair seemed mere shadows of his own. His gem gleamed in the light, as if trying to rouse its companions from slumber.

Aden remembered how proud he and Khodi had been when they were honored with their blades. Once accepted by a knight, trainees had their weapons forged. The whole experience had been humbling. They'd been given the opportunity to observe the powers of ancient beings that surpassed anything they'd known. Back then, he'd never imagined having to lay a friend's blade to rest. Their duties involved facing dangers, but it wasn't until Cormell's death and the recent brutal encounters that Aden realized how mortal they all really were. Under Cormell's tutelage, there had been instances when their lives were put on the line, but the guardian had always been there, and they'd always made it out alive. Until *that* day. It put the world into perspective for him. It wouldn't always be all right. That people could be hurt, and he could die. Aden felt that realization should scare him, but it didn't. It only strengthened his resolve to do everything in his power and to think things through before acting. All anyone could do was their best, and take one day at a time.

A fond memory resurfaced in Aden's mind. It was one of the few times when they had all been together, pupils and mentors. The day they'd forged their weapons.

"Until you return."

I'm going to be as brave and strong as Keeper Nannelle one day." Khodi swept her wooden sword before her and struck a pose.

"Don't swing that in here, there's little room for such foolishness," Knight Freesha said in a displeased tone. Her trainee's shoulders slumped, and the girl slid the weapon back to her side.

"Don't be so hard on her." Guardian Cormell chuckled. "It's an exciting day for them, and they are still young."

"Under my guidance, she will learn discipline. The sooner the better."

As the knights continued their conversation, Aden leaned

over and whispered to Khodi. "I think you're already brave to learn from that lady."

Khodi flashed him a smile but said nothing further. A handful of others were with them as they descended into the ground. On the surface, they had gotten an entire view of the structure that now moved them through the soil. It reminded Aden of a tomb and was as large as a small room. Everything was made of stone, and there were no windows. When the group had been shown the construction, Guardian Cormell had been the first to comment on it.

"I hope no one is afraid of small spaces."

Keeper Nannelle had been the one to explain what was to take place before they left, and Aden replayed her words in his mind. "The titans have constructed this to bring you far underground. There, they will forge your weapons. Don't be afraid, they will not harm you, but be respectful. For guidance, your mentors will accompany you."

Titans. Aden recalled his lessons about these ancient beings. Those who considered themselves allies to the Avant Guard had shared their history, but little else was known about them beyond that. The titans were the first to know this world, creatures of living elements. Rock titans existed before all others, the eldest of their brethren. Then the Fire erupted out of the darkness, and there were great wars waged over Mythreth. It wasn't until the dragons arrived that a victor was determined. The dragons had come from their own realm, accompanied by the Water and Wind titans. The Rocks had raised floating plateaus of earth to protect the dragons from the fighting, but eventually the Fires were subdued with the combined strength of Rock and Water, forever pledging to keep the Fire at bay.

Aden rubbed his cool hands together. He tried his best not to stare, but it was his first time meeting a titan. A Wind was among them, standing calmly in the center of the chamber. It took the form of a man, but had no distinguishable features. No eyes, mouth, nose, ears, or clothing. He couldn't even tell if it was male or female, if any such difference applied for these beings. Within its shape, a quiet storm was continually changing, pushed by unseen winds. When the titan spoke, its words were heard through his mind. It joined them on this journey, to provide air while below the surface, and to keep the heat at bay.

Aden managed to peel his eyes away and concentrated on the sound of the chamber moving through the ground. He shuddered to imagine the amount of dirt above their heads. If it weren't for the Rocks guiding their passage, they surely would be crushed.

Other than the titan, there wasn't much to see as they traveled. They had brought magic-fueled lamps with them, which chased away the darkness. He was glad to leave the chamber when they finally reached their destination. The group, along with the Wind, entered a larger space that resembled a cave. The Wind remained at the doorway, but Aden felt the cool air of the room pick up speed until there was a gentle breeze. At the very edges of their light, Rocks formed from the ground. Aden noted the differences among them. Some were wide and bulky, with many stones making up their form. Others were like the Wind, having a smooth body, devoid of imperfections. They also had no features, their words heard telepathically.

The voice was a rumble. *"The Fires come."*

A golden orange glow brightened the cave as lava slowly seeped into the seven elevated pools against the walls. The chamber warmed instantly, but the Wind worked to keep the temperature comfortable for its mortal companions.

From each pool a hand of lava emerged slowly, seeming to reach out as if grasping for something. The bulkier Rocks went and stood at the walls as silent guards. Their smooth brethren each went to stand before a pool and clasped the hand of lava. They became changed, transformed into figures of rock-armored lava. All the kits gasped in awe.

"We are the Seven." They spoke together. *"Come forward and receive our gifts, through promises of old."*

From these words, Aden was reminded of the stories of long ago, of how the ancestors of the Order had helped the titans. In return, they and following generations were honored with weapons fashioned by the creatures. Aden walked to a pool while closely guided by Cormell. He gawked at the titan, eyes wide and mouth agape.

"What is desired?" the titan asked.

Cormell cleared his throat to bring Aden out of his stupor. Aden fumbled with the wooden sword at his side and presented it to the ancient being.

The Avant Guard permitted that their recruits only wield weapons made of strong wood. The edges were dull, but the material sufficiently strong and light that they were able to train. By this time, they were experienced enough that they wouldn't accidentally harm themselves, or others, with real blades. All trainees were allowed to choose their desired weapon, or the one they showed most promise with. The sword was common, but it was what Aden preferred above all else. His weapon lifted from his fingertips and was caught up in an unnatural current of warm air. He felt the tingle of magic; then the titan turned, and the sword followed to meet the forge.

Aden leaned over and whispered to Cormell. "What's happening?"

"The titan will use your training weapon as a template. The wood was already crafted to accommodate your unique needs and style of fighting."

Aden flinched from an unexpected yank of a hair and the sting that accompanied it. "Ow! Hey!" He rubbed his head.

"Sorry about that, but they'll need this to make the crystal." Cormell let the strand be swept away in the air. Oddly, it remained floating near the titan.

"Well... what do they do if the person has no hair?" Aden asked.

The guardian chuckled. "Anything of the body could be used, but hair is the most convenient. Perhaps in that case an eyelash, nail clipping, drop of blood, or some other."

Aden tried to stop the fit of laughter that overcame him, but it still escaped in a snort.

Cormell raised a questioning eyebrow until Aden reluctantly answered. "Booger."

The guardian blinked at him in shock, but a guilty smile spread across his face. "I was trying hard not to suggest that, but truthfully, I thought the same thing when I was your age."

"Oh, grow up," Freesha snapped from her station.

She heard that? Her hearing was surprisingly acute for an older woman. Aden could imagine the anxiety Khodi felt about having her as a mentor. He truly felt pity for his friend.

The sound of heated metal sizzled and hissed behind the titan. It spun toward them, and the strand of Aden's hair floated between its hands. The creature clasped its hands together, and light escaped between its fingers. The presence of magic felt ever stronger, almost tangible, like static. Aden gasped from the spectacle and the pressure of power on his senses.

Then a piercing pain shot through him. He couldn't pinpoint it to anywhere specific in his body, but deep inside, somewhere hard to place. He knew where it came from, though, recalling a lesson in his studies. He'd never experienced it firsthand before, and was only aware of it through description from others. Traces of his soul were being torn from him! If it wasn't for Cormell's support, his knees might have buckled. He clenched his teeth while he endured the agony. Then, as quickly as it occurred, it was gone. The light from the titan's hands faded, and it turned back to its work.

"Steady there." He heard the sympathy in the guardian's words. "It's over."

Aden took a breath. "What was that?"

"The titan used your contribution to bind the weapon to your life. When you die, the magic will be undone. In a sense, it will die too. Then, as is custom, it will be returned to the fires whence it came. It's what makes our weapons unique to our Order. The titans are the utmost masters of their craft, shaping the finest steels while infusing them with magic connected to our very being."

"You could have warned me!"

"I don't think anything could have prepared you for that." Cormell patted Aden's shoulder.

"Well, let's not do that again."

"It's uncommon for a blade to be reforged, but not unheard of." Cormell smiled. "Just be thankful you chose only one blade rather than two. Those who have multiple weapons must go through the same ritual for each one."

Aden shuddered at the thought. As he recovered from the experience, he heard the pitiful gasps, grunts, and small cries from his fellow trainees. He wanted to go to Khodi, to make sure she was all right, but he was unsteady himself. He knew she would get little sympathy from Freesha. Sometimes he thought the knight could be a heartless shrew.

Then the titan turned back to face them. *"It is done."*

The blade in its hands made all of Aden's discomfort disappear. The sword was just as magnificent as Cormell's weapon, sleek and perfect. The crystal gleamed with a life of its own within the hilt. Aden couldn't help but cringe when his fingers touched the metal, expecting it to be hot from the forge. But unbelievably, the steel was cool on his skin. It was also lighter than he'd imagined, needing little effort to lift. The titan had even used the wood and leather grip from his training weapon to complete the masterpiece.

"Be careful now," Cormell warned. "It may feel as sharp as an ordinary blade to you, but is actually much more so."

Aden tested his sword through the air and noticed the other kits getting familiar with their own weapons as well. A staff was among them, an uncommon yet not unheard-of choice. Khodi brandished her very own sword, but sheathed it immediately after Freesha spoke to her.

"Why is Freesha always a grump?" Aden asked.

Cormell joined in to peer at the woman. "She's never lost a kit because they are so rigorously trained. She has molded many exceptional knights. Freesha may be stern, but is fiercely dedicated to the Order."

Once all the titans were done with their work, they each sank a hand back into the lava. The Fires left them, and they were whole Rock again. *"Until you return,"* they intoned together, and merged back into the floor.

The ceremony concluded, so they all headed back to the surface. When the Wind titan stepped into the open air, it dispersed without a sound. Aden watched as it vanished, and hoped that one day they could learn more about the mysterious beings.

While the knights discussed the outcome of their journey, the kits eagerly huddled together to show off their new armaments. Aden saw Khodi step away from the group and plant the end of her blade into the ground. She then stood back to admire it in the sunlight as Aden put his weapon next to hers. He heard the excited whispers quiet as the other trainees, one by one, followed suit.

"Too bad it won't see as much use as yours," Khodi said.

He looked at her. "What do you mean?"

She smiled sweetly, but her tone had a competitive edge to it. "Since I'm better at magic."

"Are not!" Even as he said it he knew she was right, though he hated to admit it. He doubted that any enemy would be able to get close enough to her that she'd need her sword.

"Don't worry, I'll let you have a rematch when we get back."

"You're on."

He returned her smug grin, and they continued to admire their weapons. They enjoyed the peace until their mentors were ready and it was time for further training.

A butterfly landed on the cross-guard of the sword, joining the others of its kind that had already found their place there. It basked in the light, and was only aware of the delightful sun on its wings, and the warmth of its perch.

It had no knowledge of the circumstances of the rooted weapon beneath it, nor of the blade next to it. It was oblivious to the empty depression in the ground where a sword had been, and to the silent figure leaving the gardens behind.

18

THE UNEXPECTED VISITOR

"Surely it couldn't be so bad."

Ohn'na had taken charge in the aftermath of the battle in the ruins, and was given the honor of leading the burial service. Her words carried across the courtyard, lifting like the flames of the pyre behind her. "In memory of our friends, we light this fire. Let them see it from the arms of the Divine, and know that they are in our thoughts. They fought bravely in their last hours and will never be forgotten." The gathering of knights copied her as she raised her blade in salute.

"Never be forgotten." Aden's voice mingled with the others, and after a few moments of silence, Ohn'na addressed the crowd once more.

"Those who wish to share any stories may come and do so."

Aden leaned against the back wall of the courtyard where he observed the commemoration. The sun was past its peak now, as the day wound down. Some of the injured had already been sent back to Longshield Citadel, but those who remained had insisted on staying for the funeral. The healers had arrived after the battle and were tending to the wounded who were unable to be moved. Those who couldn't be saved would be returned to the citadel and have their own funeral service.

As the first person approached the pyre to speak, Aden pushed off the wall and took his leave. He needed some time away from the ruins and found a place outside the crumbling walls where he could look across the land surrounding them. The sentries were guarding their posts, charged with the task of warning the camp of any danger. Aden considered relieving one of them, but decided against it, preferring to let his mind wander than to stay alert.

His eyes shifted from the knights on duty to the stretch of small forest in the distance. Beyond that was a region known as the Bloody Plains, relentlessly defended and controlled by the orcs and their various clans. Far to the northwest stood the High Peaks and its community of dwarves. The mountains were barely a bump on the horizon, a true testament to the vast distance. He only knew of it from the topographical lectures in his studies. Aden's mind was still far away when he heard a voice behind him.

"Are you all right?"

Aden's mind snapped back like a rubber band, and he didn't bother to turn to see who it was. "I will be."

Frafnar approached and stood next to him without another word. Aden relaxed, and was glad he wouldn't need to share the details of his grief. Frafnar remained by his side and appeared as captivated by the scenery as he was.

After a time, Aden interrupted the silence. "So... I hear you will be stationed at Orian Citadel."

"So I'm told."

"Will it be strange to work within the Order again?" It was hard for him to imagine ever being apart from it.

"I won't have to constantly watch my back. It'll be a good change, but some habits will be hard to break," Frafnar replied.

Aden nodded slowly while he reflected on what Frafnar had been through. When Aden had stumbled through the portal and borrowed the man's identity, he'd gotten a glimpse into the world that the man had survived in. Frafnar had endured that unnerving environment for years, even thriving in it. Aden couldn't help but wonder if Frafnar's promotion to captain was due to the man's cunning and skill or if the demose had played a role. "And what about the demon?"

Frafnar's sidelong look was hard to read, but then he turned back to the horizon. "I have it under control."

"What did the keepers say?"

"They're uneasy, but my situation may become useful again. For now, I'll be under close surveillance, no doubt. How could they even consider another alternative? They gave me this assignment, and their mistrust is my reward."

Aden could hear the bitterness, and Frafnar glanced at him

as he continued. "Few survive the purging. For them to need-lessly risk my life when it may be needed again would be... foolish. I'm fine as I am, so they won't press the issue."

"Aren't you worried the demon might overwhelm you?" Aden asked, recalling the struggle Frafnar had faced before the attack on Orian Citadel. He'd managed to distract his friend, but what would have happened if he hadn't been there?

"It's possible," Frafnar answered. "But in that case, the keepers will do what they must."

"What if you hurt someone before they act?"

"If I didn't know better, I'd think you're trying to convince me to rid myself of the demose, despite the danger." Frafnar gave him a wry grin. "I'm able to keep the monster at bay. That's why the keepers chose me. If you're searching for the silver lining to this, at least there's one less demon to terrorize anyone."

If death was a possibility, he could understand. Now Aden knew the truth, the keepers had asked Frafnar to do it, so for them to insist that the man risk his life to undo it would be wrong.

He couldn't help but wonder if he'd do the same if they ever asked him. He doubted they would, though. Frafnar was unique, his orc heritage giving him the edge to resist the demon. To Aden, it would be a betrayal of Khodi's trust in him. Aden was glad he didn't have a demon whispering dark things in his mind. "I'm sorry, I didn't mean to push. I wanted to understand."

Frafnar sent him another sly grin. "Don't worry about it. The demon has suggested multiple ways I could dispose of you." Aden's eyes widened, and Frafnar only laughed. "That was a joke."

"A bad one."

"Look there." Frafnar pointed down the hill. "We have a visitor."

A lone figure was approaching. From his height, Aden would've assumed it was a child, but the broad shoulders gave away his true identity. "A dwarf? Out here?"

"Let's join the sentry to meet him."

Frafnar was already sprinting down the hill before Aden could answer, but his curiosity drove him to follow. The pair made it to the sentry before the dwarf did. As the visitor got closer, they saw that he was covered in dirt, so much so that a dark layer plastered his clothing and armor head to toe. He had a hand pressed against a wound on his arm, blood dripping past his fingers. A helmet covered the face, and glyph magic shimmered across the material covering the eyes and mouth.

"Halt!" the sentry said. "The Avant Guard is camped here, state your business."

The newcomer spoke in the native dwarven language. When Aden and his companions exchanged looks of confusion, the dwarf removed the helmet. A mix of gold and gray strands of hair caught the light of the late midday sun. "My people need your help." She tried again in the common tongue.

"A dwarf woman?" The sentry voiced all their thoughts. "I expected a man."

The visitor rolled her eyes. "There's no time for this!"

"I'm sorry." Aden directed the words to the visitor, as he

deliberately stepped on the guard's toes. The sentry took a step back and lowered his eyes.

"What's the trouble?" Frafnar asked.

The woman took a second look and fear flashed in her eyes. "An orc!" She drew a knife from her belt, but even as she took a step forward, her energy was spent. Her knees buckled, and Aden reached to catch her. Frafnar wisely kept his distance, though a grim expression plastered his face.

"He's a friend, a knight of the Avant Guard, and is only part orc." Aden explained, while steadying the dwarf.

"Does your Order accept anyone now?" The woman commented weakly. "Even those such as *him*."

"It's all coming back to me." Frafnar frowned. "Now I remember why I agreed to my last mission."

The renegades accepted any heritage, and invited the masked man with no background to join them. Even if they had known he was an orc, they would have welcomed him. It wasn't a secret that orcs allied themselves with the demose. Between the different tribes, Frafnar's people were more reasonable compared to their cousins. It was widely known that the orcs worked with the Enclave, nations of the north that were ruled by the Remnents. Slavery, oppression, and a revered ideology of demons were common practices there, contrary to the principles of its southern neighbors. The people of the southern kingdoms were not only wary of orcs because of this, but also due to their aggressive and unpredictable nature.

On occasion, there were some who had no connection with their people, traveling the world and living by their own ambitions. Mix-breeds of orc and other races weren't unheard of, but fared little better—if not worse—than their brethren. Life was difficult for either if they chose to live in the southern kingdoms, having to face the prejudice and abuse from the people there. Mix-bloods had the hardest lives. The orc tribes wouldn't accept them, considering them weak, tainted, and unworthy to walk among their people. At best, they would be driven out—at worst, they'd be killed. They fared better in the south, but often faced hostility, such as the animosity toward Frafnar by the dwarf woman. Sometimes the feelings were based only on rumors, but some were from firsthand experience of the ruthlessness they encountered. Even as a member of the Avant Guard, Aden was certain that Frafnar wasn't able to escape the scrutiny and doubt of others.

"Please tell us what happened," Aden encouraged the woman as he sat her down gently on the ground and inspected her wound.

The dwarf still kept an eye on Frafnar but nodded. "I'm part of an expedition to excavate and survey beneath the Bloody Plains."

"The lands controlled by the orcs?"

"Yes. There are vast untapped resources there, as well as links to our past before the orc territory expanded. Our king believes that the reward is well worth the risk. With the help of the titans, we made it this far, but we grew too careless. The orcs found us. From what Rocky told me, they were able to reach us through natural underground caverns. It didn't take them long to dig their way into our tunnels, and by that time it was too late. They overcame us without warnin', no time to put up resistance. Though how they knew we were there, I don't know."

"Rocky?" Aden asked as he wrapped her arm with a bandage.

"A titan that seemed to take a likin' to me, as far as I could tell anyway. I guess it could have just been doin' what titans do —ouch!"

"Sorry." Aden cringed with her as he finished securing the cloth. "The wound is deep and you've lost a lot of blood already. I need to heal it. I'll give you something to ease the discomfort."

"Just stop the bleedin'," the woman said. "We don't have time."

As Aden applied a paryl pick to the dwarf's arm, Frafnar spoke. "This could start a war. Does your king not realize what that could mean?" Frafnar paced back and forth. Aden hadn't seen him so troubled before.

"The orcs have already found us. There's no turnin' back." The woman winced from Aden's healing despite the pain suppressant.

"Surely it couldn't be so bad," the sentry said. "Why would the orcs care if the dwarves ventured beneath their lands? I've not heard of orcs having an interest in the ground."

"No, but they are fearsome warriors. And they take trespassing into their territory very seriously, no matter the means. What's worse"—Frafnar shook his head in disbelief—"is that they have passed into the lands controlled by the crimsons. They are the most unreasonable and unpredictable. Even where we are now, this abandoned citadel is probably within their borders."

The sentry licked his lips and looked around, as if expecting an orc to appear at any moment. "And there's a large plume of smoke from the funeral…"

"Giving away our position," Frafnar finished the sentence.

"I've stopped the bleeding." Aden joined the dwarf in a sigh of relief as he finished.

"Good," the woman said. "Now I can take you to where I escaped, before the orcs find it."

19

ROCKSLIDE

"No offense, but I'm sure glad I'm staying here."

Frafnar carried the dwarf on his back, as he'd done for Aden earlier. The woman had refused at first, but Frafnar was the strongest among them. Reluctantly she'd agreed, after they convinced her that they'd be able to get there faster with his help.

"So, you never told us your name," Aden said as they ran. *I can't keep calling her the dwarf, the woman, or the dwarf woman in my head.*

"I'm Amell, of the Thach clan."

"How did you escape the orcs anyway?" the sentry asked. He had accompanied them to report the situation and escort the woman back to camp once she showed them the way.

"I was workin' alone in my own branch of tunnels when

they attacked. I'd heard someone approach, but I was so busy with my work I'd assumed it was one of my kin to check up on me. My pick had gotten wedged and I was gettin' it out when the orc grabbed my shoulder. My tool dislodged and the momentum caused the end to strike him behind me. He retaliated, probably thinkin' I did it on purpose. He took a stab at me with his blade, and caught my arm. If it wasn't for Rocky, I'd probably be dead. The ceilin' caved in on the orc's head. It sealed me in my tunnel, and made the orc's death look like an accident." Amell repositioned her arms around Frafnar's shoulders.

"Then Rocky explained the situation to me. The orcs had taken my people prisoner, threatenin' that if any tried to escape, they'd start the killin'. The other titans left to alert my king to what happened, but I don't know how long it will take for reinforcements to arrive. Since I wasn't discovered, and Rocky knew that the Avant Guard were close by, I set out to ask for your help. Luckily, you had the smoke goin' so it wasn't hard to find you. The sooner we can free the prisoners, the better."

"We may be the closest, but not in the best condition to lend aid," Aden said. "We just made it through a battle of our own."

"With the orcs?"

"No... It's a long story."

Amell nodded. "Well, any help you could provide would be welcome. Even if just a diversion, until my people arrive."

"If the orcs haven't killed them, what are they doing?"

Amell shook her head, having no answers.

"If you followed the smoke to us, the orcs will too. If they find the Order camped within their borders, there will be bloodshed."

"Yes, and when we return, we'll warn your people of the danger," the dwarf promised.

The group spoke little more as they traveled, and remained vigilant for any sign of orcs. Fortunately, no trouble found them, and Aden could tell he wasn't the only one relieved when Amell finally pointed at some inconspicuous boulders. Frafnar unloaded his burden and worked out the muscles of his arms and shoulders.

"Let's not make a habit of this."

Amell pointed out the hidden hole in the ground to the others. "This is where I escaped." She looked around and added, "Rocky, where are you?"

The sentry wiped his sweaty brow on his sleeve and sat on a boulder. He was taking a drink from his waterskin when the earth beneath him started to shake. Water sprayed from his mouth as he scrambled from his seat. The Rock shrank and reshaped into a smaller version of the titans Aden had seen.

"There you are. Do you have any news?" Amell's tone was urgent.

"Why don't the titans help free your people?" the sentry interrupted while he wiped the moisture from his chest. "They could save them so easily."

The words formed in their minds. *"We do not involve ourselves with the wars of mortals. We may give indirect aid, but we will not kill for them."*

"Then what can you tell us?" Frafnar asked.

"The ones you call orcs are using the smaller ones to mine the stone. They now have a Fire making weapons below."

"A Fire titan? Why would it help them?"

"The Fire wants to be freed to the surface, which the orcs have promised. They do not understand the danger. And without a Rock's help, the metal will be inferior to your weapons."

Amell took a step back as the gravity of the situation hit her. "But still better than most. Even if reinforcements arrived, they'd face superior steel. We need to stop them!"

"Why doesn't the Fire titan simply leave on its own?"

"Rocks will stop it," the titan rumbled. *"We will not allow it to leave. It hopes to find a way where we cannot interfere."*

"There was no titan before the orcs came. This is troublin' news." Amell's forehead creased.

"Could they have summoned or called it somehow?"

The titan used its power to gather sand in the air to make a map of the tunnels below. Rocky pointed to the deepest part where a jagged line connected with the main cavern. *"The Fire seeped through this fracture to reach them."*

"It doesn't matter *how*," Frafnar cut in. "Right now we are more concerned with freeing the dwarves. What can you tell us about that?"

"There are, or were," Amell added, "two dozen of my kin and a handful of human workers."

Aden studied the map as the titan revealed the positions of the captives. "They all seem to be in pairs and spread throughout the tunnels."

"Yes, and a guard for each."

"Gettin' them out without havin' their captors on your tail might be tricky." Amell tapped her chin in thought; then she wagged a finger in the air. "Unless we create a diversion. As I recall, the titans told us to stop extendin' a certain tunnel because it was gettin' too close to a lake and its aquifers, yes?" She looked to Rocky for confirmation, who nodded and expanded the map to display the nearby lake.

"The distance doesn't seem too far... would an explosion cause the tunnels to flood?" Aden asked.

"Yes. A Water is there also, eager to fight the Fire."

Amell turned to the men. "If the Water titan comes through after the explosion, you won't want to be in its way. Before the Rocks helped us, we had a lot of trouble with tunnels floodin'. When a titan was involved, even more so."

"Trigger the explosion from a distance. Got it."

Amell examined the map as the titan projected how the water would fill the tunnels. She pointed at the shaft connecting the one she was working in to those that would be flooded. "Rocky, if you blocked this passage, then my people could escape the same way I did."

"First, we'd have to get them past the orcs without being detected."

"The workers are at rest now. The orcs are now gathered in small groups."

"Then this is the best time." Amell dropped a fist into an open palm. "Rocky, if you inform my people of the plan, they'll be ready."

"Okay, hold on. Let me get this straight." The sentry waved his hand then counted off each step on his fingers. "So you get below, through this hole. Find the chamber near the lake and plant explosive runes. Find all the prisoners and get them past the orcs. Then detonate the explosion while you escape. And do all this in the dark... and all before the dwarves are forced back to work? What could possibly go wrong?"

"Oh, you know, crushed by cave-ins, drowning, gutted by orcs. The usual." Frafnar smirked.

"That reminds me." Amell handed Aden her helmet. "Use this to disguise yourself as a worker, and its enchantment by the Rocks will allow you to see in darkness. If you use light, the orcs will see you comin' and know somethin's wrong."

Aden looked at the helmet in his hands then back at the dwarf. "But there's only one—"

"I don't need one." Frafnar put his mask on to make his point.

Aden hesitated. He didn't want Frafnar to use it, but said nothing. Now was not the time for a debate.

"No offense, but I'm sure glad I'm staying here."

"Well, someone has to do it." Aden prodded the sentry with a finger to the ribs.

Frafnar moved to the opening of the hidden hole. "I'll go first." As his foot touched the tunnel floor, however, he lost his balance. Aden heard his surprised cry gradually quiet as he slid into the depths.

"Oh, yeah, better watch that first step." Amell's laugh sounded a bit maniacal.

Aden placed the helmet on his head and spoke to the sentry. "Report the situation to Ohn'na as soon as possible. Hopefully, our people leave before the orcs know they are there. And if all goes well, Frafnar and I will save the dwarves. Hurry, because as Amell said before, we don't have much time."

He then turned and followed his friend into the hole. The helmet allowed him to view the tube of rock as he slid down. He briefly wondered how the dwarf had made it to the surface, but then realized that the titan must have reformed the passage. The slide was a faster way to go down. He just hoped that throughout their time below, Rocky wouldn't abandon them. For now, he did all that he could do. He waited for the slide to end.

20

———

DANGER ON THE HORIZON

"There's activity to the south."

The orc raised his hands in reluctant defeat. He grabbed the mug before him and took a long hearty drink, draining the contents in large gulps. The dwarven ale burned as it slid down his throat. The taste was strong and overpowering, just the way he liked it. If he had to give the dwarves any credit, it was to the potency of their spirits.

One of his companions bellowed a laugh. "Better luck next time, Tork."

The winner of the round wrapped his beefy arms around the treasure, coveting the addition to his pile of riches. Tork's pile had diminished to nothing while the other three had grown plump. The remainder of the game would continue between them.

Tork slammed his mug on the makeshift stone table. He imagined planting a fist into the nearest smirking face, and he would have done so if his bladder hadn't needed tending to. Instead, he pushed away from the table and stomped away, grumbling curses beneath his breath. Maybe he'd challenge the others once he returned. He knew that the treasures didn't belong to any of them, but would be added to the riches of the tribe instead. Despite that, he still hated to lose.

Tork left the large alcove they used during rest periods. It had been designated as a storage space by the dwarves, but was now used as a gathering area for his people. He had no trouble navigating the pitch-black tunnels, his eyes able to pierce the darkness. One of the many latrines was not far, and he headed for it. As he rounded a bend he almost plowed through two human workers walking the opposite way. They were supposed to be resting; why would they risk wandering around without permission?

"Wha—?" Tork began but the air around him changed, canceling any words he could form.

One of them was able to use magic and dared to use it against him? He grabbed the closest human, the one wearing the dwarven helmet and wrapped his fingers around the throat and started to slowly squeeze. He'd show them what happened to slaves when they resisted. And if they wanted silence, he'd ensure this one would never make a sound again.

The human flailed, clawed, and pounded at his tightening grip. Tork didn't rush, wanting the other slave to watch as his friend died slow and painfully. He reserved no pity for humans. Their ancestors had the same opportunity as his to join with the demose. Too bad that they chose poorly. Humans were weak and frail compared to his people.

He was taken off guard when the second human took two large steps forward and stopped just to Tork's left side. The human made a quick movement, which pushed Tork forward slightly from his back. He looked down and saw the tip of a blade protruding from his chest, his blood dripping from the end of it. He dropped the human he was choking and watched as the blade disappeared back through him. The blood flowed freely from the wound and escaped his mouth when he coughed. He took a step forward into a darkness that swallowed him. A darkness of no return.

Frafnar cleaned the length of his sword, then returned it to his side. The quick action of Frafnar summoning the noise-canceling field had prevented them from being detected. Aden coughed and dragged in huge breaths of air. He rubbed his neck and felt the discomfort of wrenched skin under his touch. The bruising would heal; he was happy to be alive.

"*Are you all right?*" Frafnar asked for a second time that day. Aden heard the words from the verge stones they used to communicate telepathically. They'd fastened the stones to the back of their hands with fabric so they could freely carry out their task without the burden of holding them.

Aden was glad he didn't need to speak at the moment. He could imagine how hoarse his voice would be. "*Still breathing, thanks to you. I owe you one.*"

Frafnar looked at the orc near his feet. *"We'll need to hide the body."*

It didn't take them long to find a nook down one of the connecting passages. It was out of the way and served well as a hiding place. Aden struggled to help move the dead weight, and even Frafnar had difficulty.

"Where is that titan when you need it?" Aden asked mentally.

"Apparently too busy to help us take out the trash."

Aden knew the other man couldn't see the surprise on his face past the helmet, but he wished he could. Many feared and hated the crimson orcs, but he hadn't expected such views from Frafnar. He said no more. This was not the time to pry.

When they were free of their burden, they reviewed their progress. So far, they'd been able to place the explosive runes and get all the prisoners that were in the direct path of the flooding past their guards.

"We should clear the rest of the tunnels quickly," Frafnar said. *"We don't know when the dwarves will return to work, and the orcs may wonder where their buddy went."*

Ohn'na joined with two healers, and their hands hovered above the injury before them. They concentrated, pouring all their energy into the healing while the guardian helped to augment their powers and close the wound. The damage was severe, but with multiple sessions they'd been able to save the man. He was unconscious, and she was grateful for the small mercy. The suffering from the mending would have been grievous. After a time, the healers sat back and Ohn'na sighed with relief.

"For now, he's stable. He can be transported to the citadel where more can be done for him," one of the menders informed her.

Ohn'na thanked the healers before they left to tend to other patients. She stayed, needing time to recover. Ohn'na didn't have the menders' expertise or stamina. On the critical cases she assisted them, but most of the seriously injured were saved due to the talents of the master healers.

When the funeral had concluded, she'd arranged groups to evacuate to Longshield Citadel through the portals. Ohn'na looked around at the bodies covered with cloth. Some of the injuries had been beyond their power. The bodies would be brought to the citadel for their own funerals.

She realized she hadn't seen Aden or Frafnar since the ceremony and wondered where they'd gone off to. She was about to go look for them when she heard an unexpected voice call out to her.

"Ohn'na! When this lad told me you were the go-to gal, I hardly believed him. I knew you'd joined the Order, but I never would've expected you'd be here, and runnin' things no less!"

Ohn'na cracked a smile. "Aunt Amell! What are you doing here?"

"Uh, you two know each other?" the sentry asked as he looked back and forth between them.

"She's my niece, but there's no time to go into that right

now!" Amell then quickly delved into the details of what had happened.

"Crimson orcs?" Ohn'na couldn't hide her concern. She turned to the sentry. "On the way to your post, spread the word that we'll be leaving shortly."

"What of the injured?" the sentry inquired, glancing at the unconscious man resting nearby.

"If the orcs are around, it won't be long before they investigate these ruins. We must leave before that. It's better to risk moving the wounded than allowing them to be easy pickings," Ohn'na replied. "Be sure to inform the others to remain vigilant."

The sentry nodded and was about to leave when Amell placed a hand on his arm. "Thank you, lad. If I don't see you again, I want you to know that I appreciate your help." The sentry grinned and bowed before he hurried off to his duties. Amell turned to Ohn'na. "Does this mean we won't be gettin' any more help from your Order?"

"If it's as you say, our first priority is to evacuate our people. The only able bodies we have are the sentries, and they're no force to repel an orc attack. I could request more aid from the keepers, but that would take time. I'm not certain if they'd risk a confrontation with the recent casualties. I believe all we can do is wait and hope that Aden and Frafnar can get the captured dwarves and humans to safety, and that your people arrive soon."

The orc squinted, to see as far as he could with his good eye. The sun was already well past high time, and he had received word that smoke was rising from the long-abandoned ruins to the south. As hard as he tried, there was no sign from this distance. His fortifications were stationed on the opposite side of a lake in relation to the disturbance on the borders of their lands.

"There's activity to the south."

Roxx didn't need to see the woman who spoke next to him. She'd chosen to stand on his blind side, like many of his challengers. The vessel the demose chose was of a young elven woman, easy prey to possess. To her people, she would have been considered attractive, but he couldn't understand why the demon would choose such a frail body. He knew the demose was anything but weak, however. She could display a strength greater than his own if she so wished. In small, subtle ways, she liked to remind him that she was his superior, such as now when she stood at his seemingly vulnerable side.

Roxx prided himself on having the disadvantage yet still remain chief, able to best any orc who challenged him. He'd lost his right eye in his battle with the previous leader but had triumphed in the end. He was big, cunning, and intelligent enough to rein in his zeal when necessary. That combination, as well as adapting to his blindness, had been the reason he'd kept his station for so long. He'd led this region for thirty seasons now, longer than most orcs ever held the title of chief. And even though he knew better than to try, there were many times he imagined snapping the neck of the deceptively frail elf. He served the Ancient One, not this demon pawn. She was the eyes and ears for his master, and until that changed he'd remain subdued. Roxx despised her, but he knew his place and wisely kept these feelings to himself.

"Perhaps we should have established the fort in the old ruins, as you suggested long ago," the demose continued. "As I recall, you argued the tactical benefit as well as the trophy rights to the conquered land."

Another test. Despite the many years he'd served with her, she still enjoyed toying with him. To her, he answered tactfully. "We've benefited from the lake, and the nearby cavern, which was useful to reach the dwarves. Your advisement was the right course." He'd been wise enough not to force his choices long ago, and so he still remained. Not only did he have to contend with challenges from his own people, but he had to watch his back with the demose as well. If she considered him a threat, she would be rid of him.

The slightest smile tugged at the corners of the elf's mouth. "Indeed."

After some time, she spoke again. "Let's go investigate; you must be eager to learn what's happening. Perhaps we'll find something to amuse us."

Roxx entertained the thought of pushing her down the battlement steps, of destroying that smug, arrogant face. His immediate execution would almost be worth it. Almost. Instead, he followed in her wake.

21

THE FURY OF GRIEF

"...when I am ready."

Knight Mariyn Freesha was the last to stand near the pyre that had been built to honor their fallen friends. The fire slowly consumed the large pile of wood gathered in the middle of the courtyard, far away from any foliage it could spread to. The flames reached high into the air, while smoke rose above like a beacon to inform all of the recent death there.

Upon Freesha's arrival at the ruins, Aden Fendrie had informed her about the fate of her trainee, Khodi Terrus. She had already known somehow, from the ache in her chest. When Aden had presented her weapon, Freesha had instructed him to place it in the gardens, where Khodi had fought her last battle. She knew her trainee would have liked that. She'd never understood the girl's excitement over flowers, but it reminded her of someone she'd known long ago.

The boy had been unable to save her, but Freesha couldn't lay the blame on him. He was a friend of Khodi's, and she was certain he'd done all he could. The sadness in his eyes alone would have erased any doubt, reflecting the deep wound in her own heart. If she was angry with anyone, it was herself, for allowing this to happen. If she had been more mindful of her kit, things might've been different. She'd saved as many as she could at Orian Citadel, but the loss of the others meant little to her. It had been her duty to do so, nothing more. She found the death of Khodi hard to accept. Like a hurricane on the high seas, she was ready to beat on anything in sight.

"The last of us are leaving through the portals, Knight Freesha. There's a report of crimson orcs nearby; we should leave quickly."

She recognized the voice of Guardian Ohn'na Sazi. Freesha struggled to keep the anger from her tone as she answered the woman. "I will follow, when I am ready."

She relaxed slightly when Ohn'na stepped away. The guardian didn't deserve her wrath. Freesha's back had been to the woman, but somehow Ohn'na must have understood her need to be alone. The more Freesha thought about Khodi's death, the more the storm built within her. She clenched her fists tightly. Soon she would need to strike out at something. It was better to find one of the many trees nearby, and deal it unwarranted punishment rather than a fellow knight.

That's when she heard the footsteps nearby. At first she

thought it was Ohn'na, returning to try and convince her to leave, but the scraping sound of a drawn weapon warned her that it wasn't an ally. It was now late in the day, and the sky had become overcast. It was the perfect reflection of her mood. She turned her head to look behind her, and the light of the fire cast shadows in her wake.

The crimson stood there, unaware of the danger. As the name suggested, his skin was a deep red, as were his eyes. The intense hatred from him might have rivaled her own. The orc was bald, and dressed with minimal armor. His muscles bulged and flexed, some veins making lines in his skin. *He's a scout, then,* she speculated. Freesha didn't really care why he was here, but just appreciated something to focus her rage on.

The orc gave a guttural growl of his own, and he threw one of his axes in her direction and charged. Freesha burst into action, faster than any her age, spinning away and dodging the axe. She spoke a couple words of power and took out a ball of leather from her pocket and threw it in the orc's path. When she reached a fallen column of stone she activated the explosive rune, which discharged needles of poison. The sound was minimal, more like a loud pop than an explosion.

The orc didn't pause. His footsteps still pounded toward her. She didn't need to peek from cover to know he was upon her. She instinctively ducked as an axe swung over her head and clanged against the stone. Freesha saw an opportunity to take out one of his legs and dove at it, only to meet a wall of muscle. She'd forgotten how formidable this race was, and this one was small compared to his brethren.

The orc barely flinched at her attempt. While she was momentarily stunned, he grabbed the clothing on her back, and with a roar, he threw her from her hiding place. Freesha rolled when she landed, leaving her cloak behind. The orc embedded his axe into the cloth as he followed her, and took another vertical swing. She used her momentum to get to her feet and threw a couple of her poisoned knives at him.

Freesha refrained from using too much magic, since orcs were largely unaffected by it. He would resist the poison as well, but it would eventually slow him down. She used her powers to enhance her own skills but kept it to a minimum to prolong her own stamina. One slip and she'd meet her end.

The knives found their mark, one in the shoulder and another in the leg, but the orc kept coming. He roared as he attacked, his blood rage allowing him to ignore the pain. She spun and blocked his axe with her blade. She fell from his strength and moved with it. There was no way she could match his brutality blow for blow. She maneuvered away from his swings, blocking and flowing with the force of it when she had to.

After a time, he stumbled forward and his weapon dropped from his grasp. The orc blinked, finally, as the poison took effect and disoriented him. Freesha used the opportunity and kicked the back of his knees, making him kneel. With one quick slice of her blade, she removed his head from his shoulders, the keen edge of her sword making smooth work of it.

The body balanced there for a few moments. Freesha's hand morphed into a dark claw and she sank it deep into the dead crimson's chest, breaking bone to the reward beneath. She retracted her arm with the heart in hand. She had not yet been able to sample an orc, and now was the perfect chance when she wanted to vent. She still had so much more to let out. It wasn't just about Khodi anymore; it was everything she'd held back since posing as a human.

Freesha ate the heart and felt the change overcome her. She was a goblin after all, and changing from the form she'd worn for so long felt strange, but more of a relief. It was like stretching muscles after a long rest.

She walked from the ruins of the citadel. Her skin morphed to a deep red; her muscles hardened and grew. Her hair darkened to a midnight black, her stature increased, and her canines grew sharper and more prominent. The whites of her eyes turned black, and her irises to red. Her armor stayed in place, stretched to its very limits. Despite all these changes, she was barely conscious of them in her eagerness to meet the enemy.

Beyond the trees, a handful of orcs approached on foot with their weapons drawn. She could tell they were assessing her—she certainly wasn't the scout they'd sent ahead—but they continued toward her.

Still gripping her weapon, she slammed it into the ground. She embedded the end of the blade far enough into the dirt to keep the weapon upright. The gem inlaid in the hilt, which normally gleamed a brilliant red, was now black. Freesha flexed her clawed fingers and gritted her teeth. She'd take them down with her bare hands; the blade would be too quick for her liking. Foolish perhaps, but she needed to. She felt the raw strength through her limbs and would use this power to show them her fury.

Without a word, she charged the orcs and met the first without pause. He'd been faster than the others, obviously younger and eager for the kill. Freesha spun and swept her leg against the orc's, breaking through the strong wall of muscles. As he fell, she leaped and stomped on his throat. He didn't rise again as she hastened to engage the others.

The remaining four orcs surrounded her but kept their distance. *Well, at least their brawn hasn't diminished their brains,* Freesha thought, amused at their caution once they'd seen how quickly she'd disposed of their comrade. She taunted the biggest of the group with a malicious smile. She waited for them to make the first move. Of course, her restraint would feel like mockery to them. They eyed her dark claws, and then saw her shoulder crest that identified her as a knight of the Order.

Four. Freesha heard a roar from the one to her left that attacked first, a signal to the others to do the same. She dodged the swing of one weapon, using her own arm to guide it to clash with another. She elbowed the one nearest her hard in the face, and pushed the orc into his fellow. She used her claws to shred flesh, penetrating far enough to break a major vein. *Three.* An errant weapon dug deep into the chest of another. *Two.* Freesha managed to strike a groin with her leg, and as the orc reflexively leaned forward, she drove her knee into his face. With both hands, she gave his head a tight twist and heard his neck break. *One.* The biggest crimson was left, and he wouldn't go down as easily. Some of his attacks connected through her defenses, but her claws finished him after a few substantial blows.

Freesha felt the release of emotion as each orc fell, but she was still at her peak and wanted more. *Just a foretaste* she thought, as she heard the roars from another group nearby, with more coming in the distance. She picked up the small axes from the dead and threw them once the new threats were in range. Two were parried, but one hit its mark in the chest. Freesha managed to handle them as well, but they were more coordinated and skillful than the last. For her efforts, she suffered a deep gash in her side, which added to the bruises and cuts she'd already received. The pain enraged her further, but her energy was draining.

One crimson still lived but kept his distance despite her injuries, waiting for more to arrive rather than take her on his own. Unwilling to chase him down, Freesha took out a knife and threw it straight into his heart. Her enemy thought he was safe with the distance between them. *Around a goblin,* Freesha thought, *never let your guard down.* She grimaced against the pain. *Especially one as evidently suicidal as me.*

She saw the others coming. Soon they'd be upon her, and it would be over. She took out a paryl pick from a pouch and jammed it into her leg. It would help her face what was to come. She'd held everything back for so long, and Khodi's death was the last straw. Fortunately for her, the orcs had come, but it appeared she'd exchanged her life for her need to unleash her fury. She didn't want to die. But what was done was done, and if that was the price to be paid, she wouldn't go down without a fight.

A hysterical grin spread across her face. She remained where she was, resolved to meet her fate head-on rather than try to flee like a coward. *So... this is how it will end. Heh. Let them come, then! I am ready!* She stood tall, and waited for the tide of death to embrace her.

22

———

REVELATIONS

"...one most wouldn't expect."

So certain of her fate, Freesha's jaw dropped when two consecutive explosions of fire rained down on the closest orcs. Two more landed deeper in the ranks of the approaching enemies, giving her time to act. The magic would stun them, but not for long. A few of the orcs made it through the barrage, but as they got closer, Guardian Ohn'na Sazi charged past her to engage them. Freesha still wore the outer husk of a crimson; why was the woman helping her?

As Ohn'na intercepted an enemy, the ground rumbled and a section of the ground exploded between her and the approaching enemy forces. Battle cries escaped the new hole, and dwarven warriors spilled from it. The orc broke off from fighting Ohn'na and turned his attention to the new threat.

Dwarves kept emerging from the ground, and a couple tackled him.

Ohn'na retreated to where Freesha stood. "We'd better leave before they think we're allied with the crimsons."

Freesha noted a couple dwarves pointing in their direction and didn't argue as she followed the guardian. She made sure to retrieve her blade and it felt good to have it at her side once more. Freesha regarded the sword with renewed reverence, resolving to limit her hand to hand combat. She glanced at Ohn'na as they headed back to the ruins, curious about what the woman would say once they reached safety. Now that the guardian knew of her origins, she doubted it would be anything good.

Aden moved as quickly as he could without sacrificing his stealth. He was to evacuate the lowest tunnels while Frafnar cleared the upper passages. He felt the air warming as he descended. The last of the dwarves were in the caverns connected to the main chamber, where the Fire titan fashioned the weapons. Aden hoped the titan would be too busy to notice them.

Up ahead, the tunnel turned a bend and Aden saw the light against the wall. He crept to the corner and removed his helmet as he took a peek. The enchantments of the helm made the light cast blindingly bright, but he tucked it under his arm for the trek back through the dark passages. Aden wiped the sweat from his brow and cautiously leaned over to get a look.

He squinted against the light of the room while his eyes adjusted to the change.

The dome-shaped cavern was immense with large columns not far from the wall, forming a circular ring inside the room. There was enough space between the wall and the columns for someone to edge around and yet remain hidden. Stone debris was piled between most of the pillars, which could provide further cover. A small pool of magma lay in the center of it all, but there was no sign of the Fire, or the Rocks.

As Aden slipped past the first column he heard activity across the cavern. After a moment of studying the rubble, he decided it was sturdy enough to climb. He realized that the debris was the leftover material from the more recent excavations. Since the Rocks no longer helped with the work, the miners had to move the excess stone themselves.

A brood of orcs entered the cavern from a passage across the room. They carried small crates on their backs and approached a mound of unfinished weapons. The metal had been forged, but the grips still needed to be added. The orcs began filling their crates.

The magma rippled and bubbled. As the Fire titan emerged, so did Rocks, rising from the ground around it. One of the orcs left the group and stepped closer to the pool to speak to the Fire, but he didn't stand too close. The orc must have faced a sweltering temperature, since Aden felt the heat even from a distance. Orcs were able to endure such extremes, more so than humans.

"I have made enough of these toys. I demand to be freed from this prison." The Fire spoke.

The orc shrugged. "That's up to the chief, and he hasn't given the order. Keep working and you'll see the surface soon."

"Too long have I heard these lies. I will be freed, now!"

The crimson backed away as the Fire raised a leg to leave the pool. "Hurry! Fill the crates, we are leaving!" he yelled as he darted to the group.

The Rock titans had remained motionless up to that point, but now burst into action. They wrestled and grabbed the Fire's arms, holding it back from continuing further.

Seeing this, the orc leader sneered. "Too bad for you. You aren't going anywhere."

Enraged, the Fire titan burned hotter. It slipped through the grasp of the Rocks holding it, and grabbed the head of a Rock in one of its hands and squeezed. The Rock's form melted away from the heat, like dough that slips through a baker's fingers. The Rock titan fell as the others hardened themselves further and jumped at their charge.

Aden was immediately aware of the evil presence, and the hairs on the back of his neck rose. The Fire titan had joined with a demon. He'd never heard of such a thing, and his mind reeled with the possibility.

"You think they will stop me?" The Fire's flames were now tinged with black. *"I will burn through them, then you all!"* The titan lifted the other leg from the pool, completely free of it now.

The Rocks holding it burned and melted, while the others bonded together to form a dome around their prisoner. They morphed into a hexagonal pattern. The Fire roared and smashed at the prison. To Aden's horror, he heard the slightest crack split within the cage.

Aden staggered back from his vantage point. He ran to the tunnel where the dwarves awaited him. He continued to hear the pounding from the Fire, but then there was a muffled thud and the ground shook. At first, Aden thought the Fire had gotten free, but again heard it banging against its confinement. Frafnar then contacted him through the verge stone.

"The runes have been set off. Was that you?"

A sinking feeling tugged at Aden's stomach. *"No. Probably the Rocks. They're having a problem down here."*

Frafnar's pause spoke volumes; no doubt he wanted to know what happened but knew there was no time for an explanation. *"You'd better hurry,"* was his only reply.

Aden knew it too. By now, Frafnar probably had the dwarves and humans heading to the surface, but Aden was still below with the water coming fast. There was a louder crack as the Fire titan continued to pound at the walls of its prison and the assault increased in rhythm. It knew the water was closing in.

When Aden reached the dwarves, they were pacing back and forth, eager to leave. "Go! *Go!*" There was no longer any need for silence, and Aden pointed to the tunnel he'd come from. The dwarves didn't hesitate and rushed for it.

Ohn'na could tell that the paryl pick did well to mask the pain, but Freesha was still mindful of the gash in her side. The knight applied pressure on her wound to stop the bleeding, but it still leaked profusely.

Once they were within the relative safety of the ruins, Ohn'na made her stop. "We'd better deal with that gash before you bleed out on me and I have to drag you back."

Freesha sat on a flat, broken piece of stone and let her begin the mending. The knight remained in her orc body, and Ohn'na guessed that she felt that it could handle the procedure better than her human form.

"That was a foolish thing to do." Ohn'na couldn't hold back the scolding and secretly regretted that all the healers had gone back to the citadel. "You could have died. Not the actions I would expect of a knight of the Order."

Freesha glared at her. "What do you care? You know what I am, why did you help me? Why *are* you helping me?"

Ohn'na thought back to when she'd overseen the last of her people leaving through the portals. She'd been very aware that Aden and Frafnar hadn't been part of that number. She understood that Aden was no longer her trainee, but she couldn't bring herself to abandon them. She'd gone back in the direction of the courtyard where she had left Freesha, intending to invite her along. Ohn'na had arrived to witness the dead orc at Freesha's feet, and her appetite for his heart. At first, she was horrified, but as she watched the woman's change, she decided to remain hidden to allow herself time to absorb what she had witnessed.

It was impossible that the keepers hadn't known about this; as for why they would accept such a creature within their ranks, she couldn't guess. Despite this knowledge, there were many times she'd wanted to help when the crimsons had attacked. The woman was still a knight, after all. But Freesha had held her own against the formidable warriors, and Ohn'na was impressed. While analyzing her behavior and ferocity, Ohn'na came to realize it was Freesha's way of mourning the loss of her kit. She never would have expected such feelings from a goblin, and it intrigued her. She supposed it was partly why the keepers granted it.

"You are a knight of the Avant Guard, and that's all that matters. You wouldn't be part of the Order if you weren't worthy of it."

Freesha arched an eyebrow. "What I am... doesn't bother you?"

"Not unless you were behind the assault on Orian Citadel. There are pieces that don't quite fit together."

Freesha stuck out her chin. "I had nothing to do with that."

"Obviously." Ohn'na gave her a little knowing smile. The most likely reason the keepers kept her origins a secret was because, when events went awry, some would be suspicious that Freesha was behind it. She remembered some of the trouble Frafnar encountered because of his heritage. Ohn'na thought the Order was better than the closed-minded view of the world, but still, some of the prejudices seeped through. "No, what I remember was that the renegade leader was one of the first to disappear when all this began."

"So she must have run off, unhappy with the Order for some reason or other."

"I don't know..." Ohn'na tried to find the connection but it eluded her. "She seemed to have a specific vendetta against me as well."

"Did you know her?"

"No. At least not well. Only heard her name mentioned in passing." Ohn'na tried to recall anything she could about the woman, but nothing memorable came to mind.

"A grudge against something unintentional then."

Ohn'na highly doubted it, but in any case, it was somewhere to start. She would begin an investigation once she returned to her duties. She managed to mend Freesha's wound enough to stop the bleeding and sat back. "That should do it for now. Just don't rip it open until it can heal."

"Yes, mother." Freesha grinned at her own cleverness as she allowed her body to change back into human form and tightened her armor so it wouldn't hang from being stretched to its limits.

"Now that I know you aren't the typical goblin, I find your roots fascinating. I too come from an unconventional background, one most wouldn't expect." She received a skeptical look from Freesha as she continued. "My father is a dwarf who loves to sing and entertain. He's a bard of sorts, which might not be too unexpected with the typical dwarven love of the drink. My mother is one of the rare druid merchants who toured the lands and traded goods with other caravans in her younger years with no responsibilities. They found each other and traveled together, and inevitably fell in love. Such is the way of the world, unpredictable at times."

"Do they still live?"

"I'm sure they're around, traveling the world. I rarely get to see them because of my work in the Order, and they never stay in one place too long. I never worry, though—they can take care of themselves. When I came along, they were proud when the Avant Guard became my life." Ohn'na noticed Freesha's faraway expression, as if she was reliving her own memories. She thought this the best time to test the waters. "So... who is Mariyn Freesha, really? Or was that a name you made up?" At some point the goblin had obtained the heart of a human, though Ohn'na hoped it hadn't been through unsavory means. But with the return of a prompt glare, she quickly added, "Ah, never mind! Forget I asked."

Now Ohn'na was more curious about the knight's past. What was the story behind it? Maybe when the wound of Khodi's death wasn't so raw, she would try again. For now, she changed the subject. "We should go see how the dwarves are faring against the orcs."

Freesha's hard stare didn't waver as she answered, "Indeed we should."

"Wait! I'm goin' back!"

----

*T*he orcs have discovered the barriers the titan placed."
Aden heard Frafnar's voice in his mind through the
verge stone. *"There's too many to confront, and only too late did
they realize the danger of breaking them. You'll have water
coming down your tunnel."*

Aden cursed his luck and stopped the dwarves before they
entered the passage. His magic tingled around them, and hid
them from sight just as orcs emerged from the darkness.

"The dwarves must have—" one was saying as he entered
the cavern, but lost his words when the titans came into view.
"Help bring the weapons to the surface!"

The orc repeated the orders as more of his kin arrived. He
continued until the water surged from the passage, sweeping

away anything in its path. More water spewed from the tunnel at the opposite side of the room, a Water titan at the head of it, like a tidal wave leading a surge of water.

"Climb for your lives!" Aden shouted over the roar of the water. He released his spell, while ignoring the cries that assaulted his ears from the orcs who'd been caught in the deadly currents.

The dwarves reappeared, and he saw them enter the tunnel. They had pick-like tools in their hands, which they anchored into the walls to prevent the water from dragging them away. Aden remembered that the dwarves had experience dealing with water, and was amazed by their agility and strength despite the forces pushing against them. Even as more orcs spilled from the tunnel, the dwarves were able to dodge the obstacles while they escaped.

Aden dropped his helmet and turned to meet the large volume of water that raced toward him from the opposite way. He veered into the entrance of the passage behind him, praying that no other orcs would come sliding out of the tunnel at him. The water that tugged at his legs wasn't as much of a concern as the waves that threatened to submerge them all. He willed the water back with his power, trying to give the dwarves enough time to escape. As he did so, he got a clear view of the titans. He observed the Fire escape its prison just as the Water titan rushed to meet it. Steam hissed while they wrestled and exchanged blows. The Rocks around them reformed the prison, while a few others moved to help the Water and merge with it to strengthen their power.

Aden held the waves at bay for as long as he could, but he

gradually weakened and they broke through. The water slammed against his body, carrying him back through the passage and away from the battling titans. He grabbed the corner of the wall, but his grip didn't hold and he was swept down an adjacent tunnel from the main passage. He felt the force of the water slam him against the wall where the tunnel ended, and he struggled to keep his head above the surface as the mine flooded. Aden tried to push off the wall, but the constant pressure against his body was too strong. By this time, the passage was almost completely submerged.

He felt panic seize him, unable to focus on anything but the cold fear. He heard whispers in his mind, demose using his terror to render a deal. It took all his willpower to order them away, to deny them from persuading him. If he didn't find a way out, he faced drowning, but even that fate was better than allowing a demon to rule him.

Now, drowning wasn't his only concern. He felt how the water temperature had increased significantly in the short time he'd been pinned. The battle between the titans, in combination with the magma pool, had heated the water at a rapid rate. Soon it would be unbearable.

An idea dawned on him, and he remembered learning of a spell that allowed him to breathe underwater. *What was it? What was it!* Aden frantically searched his memory, his fear clouding his thoughts. The water completely filled the tunnel now and his head was submerged. He held his breath while he felt like he was in a very warm bath in total darkness. Then, like a beacon of light, the spell came to mind.

He hesitated. Was he only prolonging the inevitable? If he

didn't drown he'd boil to death, and there was no way he could get free of the pressure against him. As his lungs complained from the lack of air, his instincts overrode his logic and demanded a few more precious moments. He cast the spell and gasped a large lungful of air.

From the darkness, something solid, like a shackle, wrapped around his wrist and pulled him. With the intensity of the tow he found himself flailing like a hooked fish through the submerged tunnels, against the strong forces pushing against him.

All was black, and his arm and wrist ached from the stress, until the flow of water changed abruptly and pushed against his back. The heat stung his skin now. His lungs began to burn again, until he finally broke through the surface of the water. He sputtered and coughed, heaving large volumes of air back into his lungs. After a few moments of rest, the grapple on his wrist led him through the black tunnel. Cold water pushed against him but was a relief to his hot skin.

When Aden recovered and could spare the energy, he cast the magic to see the path. The golden light emanated from his palm and brought the tunnel into focus. The water that rushed against him was only knee deep, but he heard the flooded lower passage behind him start to bubble and boil.

He was strong-armed to keep a swift pace forward and used the light to see what clenched his wrist. A titan's hand firmly held him, connected to an arm that stretched from the wall. It brought him well away from the rising water before it released him. The head of the titan emerged from the wall and

Aden suspected it was Rocky. From what he'd seen, there was no way to distinguish one titan from another.

"You saved my life." Aden rubbed his wrist and rotated his shoulder.

"Tell the dwarf Amell that I will not be coming back. Go now, before the water comes."

"But—" Aden began, but the Rock had sunk back into the stone and was gone. It was the second time he'd been saved today, and he was grateful for it. He tried to communicate with Frafnar, but the verge stone was gone, lost during his under-water escapades.

Aden was careful to ensure he didn't lose his footing from the water flowing against him. He was well aware of the hot water behind him, and he absolutely didn't want to return to it. He headed toward the surface and hoped the dwarves had made it to safety.

Amell regretted it, even as her foot touched the ground when she emerged from the portal. Ohn'na had insisted she go through to the citadel, but a feeling of unease churned her stomach. Or was that from the magic that had transported her here? She knew many who wouldn't hesitate to lay blame on the arcane arts, despite their hypocritical use of enchantments. Amell had an open mind about such things, and it was one of the reasons she had become a surveyor. Many wanted to leave the truth buried, regardless of the outcome. But there was evidence to suggest that some of their dwarven ancestors could use magic. There was no concrete proof yet, but Amell was certain an answer lay in the ruins of their past that could bring the truth to light.

Magic no longer touched her people, but that was no reason to fear and condemn it. She had once thought as her people did, but after meeting Clar'rel, her view had changed completely. Clar'rel was a druid, and her brother's wife. The woman had been the one to ignite Amell's curiosity about their past, sharing stories that could link their ancestors.

Amell had been born from architects and miners of the stone, and used her family's knowledge and connections to search for long-forgotten ruins of her people. Unfortunately, they were not the only ones to make their homes in the depths of the earth, and she was happy for the protection from the men who were friends of her late husband. Amell's mate had been one of the protectors of their city, and had died doing so. He was a brave and good man, and she knew his soul was at peace. Her twin boys had followed in their father's footsteps, so it was up to her to uncover the mystery of their past.

Her brother, Holando, wasn't much help either. He preferred the life above ground, drawn to music and adventure. It was fitting that he'd married a merchant, but Amell was surprised she was a druid, and her reaction wasn't without warrant. Druids were usually reclusive, hidden well amid the expansive wilds. Clar'rel enjoyed trading the wares of her people for things they could never find in the wilderness. Such as chocolate. Amell recalled the many times she'd found the woman enjoying those little delights.

Clar'rel and Holando were rare people among their races,

but fit so well together that none could dispute the pairing. Briefly, Amell wondered how her brother was, but she knew the answer. Happy. He was with his love, traveling and seeing the world. Whatever they faced, they'd make it through together.

"Where is Guardian Ohn'na Sazi?"

The question pulled Amell from her thoughts, and she looked at the portal guard. "She told me to inform you that she'll be joinin' us later. She will notify you when she's ready."

"Unfortunately," the guard responded, "this is the last portal for now. We have no more crystals here to open one, as they are rare to come by."

"What? Wait! I'm goin' back!" Amell turned around to step through, but it was already gone.

"Guardian Sazi knew that would be the last portal. If she stayed, she had good reason," the guard said before taking his leave.

"She didn't tell me that." Amell spoke softly to herself. She stood where the portal had been. She stared at the empty space, wishing she could bring it back with her will alone, wanting to return and help.

"You must be Amell Thach. Ohn'na has told me so much about you. I am Keeper Nannelle and I welcome you to our citadel."

When Amell turned and faced the woman, her jaw dropped. "You're a dwarf... and a keeper?"

"Yes."

Amell hurried to the older woman and clasped her hand, ensuring she was truly real. "I'd heard the rumors, but never have I met anyone of our kin who can actually use magic. I have so many questions, I don't know where to begin!"

"How about we start with some dinner, and you can ask me anything you like." Nannelle led Amell away. "Ohn'na told me of your research, and I've looked forward to meeting you."

24

TALK OF WAR

"This is the most unusual group of knights I've ever seen."

Frafnar sensed the demon stir within him, speaking as if only half-awake. *"Another demose is nearby... but of no consequence."* The demon returned to its slumber, waiting for something worthy of its attention.

Frafnar had guided the liberated dwarves to the surface, through the tunnel he and Aden had used. The Rock titan had changed it back into a walkable passage and explained that it extended far enough to bring them near the old ruins. Once they'd exited via their escape route, they were close enough to witness the fighting between the dwarves and orcs. The dwarves were fierce warriors from their own hardships, and had held their own against their larger foes. Frafnar had managed to convince the rescued dwarves to wait until he assessed the situation before they rushed to help. As Ohn'na and Freesha appeared from the ruins, Frafnar caught their attention and motioned for them to join him.

"You got the dwarves out." Ohn'na took a head count, then added, "And most of them, I see. Where's Aden?"

"Getting the last of them—" His words were lost amid the sound of a horn that blared across the plains.

"What was that?" Freesha asked, sounding a tad anxious.

"A signal to the orcs," Frafnar explained. "To regroup and reform."

"Good!" one of the nearby dwarves yelled. "We go to bolster our numbers!" This declaration was met by bellows of approval from his comrades, and they went to join their brethren, despite Frafnar's protests.

"Dwarves." Frafnar shook his head in frustration but then saw Ohn'na's rising eyebrow and added, "No offense."

In the many years he'd known her, Roxx had never seen the elf so uneasy. She would repeatedly look over her shoulder, as if an enemy might attack her at any moment. Of course, she wouldn't share her apprehension with him, and only *advised* that he recall the warriors. If it were up to him, he'd be up at the head of the battle, but it was a position that would leave him most vulnerable. He had no doubt that one fool would use the opportunity to get rid of him.

Roxx blew the horn and watched as his men and the dwarves eventually disengaged from each other. The dwarves didn't try to press them back, which meant they welcomed the respite. As the dwarves reorganized their own people, another wave joined them from the ruins. Three others followed the group, and he recognized their crests, which distinctly identified them as part of the Avant Guard Order.

"We'll speak with them before we press another attack."

In his surprise, Roxx almost fell from his horse. "In these long years, when have you ever negotiated?" The fiery glare she shot him sobered him instantly. "Fine, we talk then." His mount bounded forward and his men stepped aside to give them room to pass.

Most of the dwarves were warriors, miners, or excavators. For this reason, they elected that Ohn'na be the one to represent them in the talks. She was Amell's niece, after all, and a member of the peacekeeping Order.

Unlike the dwarves with their enchanted helmets, and the orcs with their night vision, Ohn'na couldn't see in the dark. The light of the full moon brightened the area and glinted off armor, but she used her power to create a small orb of golden light that floated nearby. She allowed her fellow knights to accompany her for support when she was to meet with the orc chief in the neutral area between the opposing sides.

"Well, well," a young elf woman said as she examined the trio. "This is the most unusual group of knights I've ever seen. A goblin, a druid-dwarf... thing, and a half-orc pup."

The orc chief spit to the side at the mention of the last

member of the group, but Frafnar didn't miss the disrespectful gesture toward him and answered in kind. "I accept your challenge, suckling."

Ohn'na had heard the word before. Suckling was the term the other orc races would call the crimsons to insult them, associating their skin with red newborn babies. Ohn'na expected the leader to lash out in rage, but surprisingly he stood firm and fought back with words.

"You are rejected by your own people, and you are definitely of no interest to me, grayback mix-blood. Count yourself lucky now, boy, but you may yet die by my hand today."

"Enough!" The elf woman gave her ally a dangerous side look. The chief averted his eyes, but as soon as it was safe, his gaze shot right back to her with hatred. "The dwarves have crossed into our lands and attacked us. For this, they must be made examples of."

"You have enslaved them in your mine below; the dwarven kingdoms will not take kindly to this," Ohn'na countered. The eyes of the elf woman unnerved Ohn'na: red, aglow, and penetrating. Although, the woman's gaze lingered on Frafnar the most.

The elf ignored Ohn'na's words and directed her question to Frafnar. "Are you here to try and usurp me?"

Frafnar's face darkened. "You are an insect. As I am to my people, you are nothing."

This seemed to anger the woman more than if he had been there to replace her. The charge in the air around her was building rapidly.

To Ohn'na, it was evident she was about to unleash a spell.

She took a step back and prepared a defensive counter. Before anyone had time to react, a dark beam of deadly magic pierced through the elf. Strands of electricity accompanied the assault and blasted the woman from her mount. The horses whinnied and reared in alarm, and the elf's horse galloped away. The chief was able to keep his mount at bay, and held his ground. The woman was motionless where she lay, her eyes open and her mouth slightly parted. She was dead, the demon gone from her. Ohn'na glanced at the body, then stared at Frafnar, where the magic had originated. He blinked several times, as if coming back to his senses. Foreseeing the danger, it appeared that the demon within him had struck like a viper and then recoiled back to its slumber.

Frafnar held up a hand to calm her, once he'd realized what happened. "It just saved our lives."

Ohn'na pursed her lips in uncertainty, but Freesha seemed unaffected by it all. Her attention remained on the chief, and what he would do next.

To the surprise of all, the orc bellowed a laugh. "You did me a great favor this day. For that I won't kill you. I won't start a war today, but war will come. I'll not lose more men against your cohort of mongrels, not until my master demands it."

With that he turned his horse and rejoined his men. They retreated, and those on horseback joined their chief to report to their master. The others stripped their dead of anything useful and left them for the beasts.

Ohn'na wasn't sure what the orc had meant about losing more men until she turned and saw the ruins. Small fires, like torches, were visible through the windows that still held form, and there were cracks in the walls and up on the fortifications. It appeared as though more troops waited inside. Ohn'na knew better, and the mystery was solved when Aden and a pair of dwarves emerged from the structure. When Aden reached them, she noticed he was soaked to the bone. His arms were wrapped around himself and he shook, but a smile lit his face.

"That was quick thinking!"

"Thank the dwarves"—Aden patted his closest companion on the back—"it was their idea."

The dwarf's smile was hard to see through the thick unkempt beard that covered his face. "Aye. A couple dwarves addin' to the mix wouldn't have been anythin' special. We wanted to trick 'em that an army was nearby, and was discussin' it when this half-drowned lad caught up to us. Unfortunately, ma'am, we had to use some of the pyre to do it."

Ohn'na shook her head. "They'd be proud that it saved more lives today."

The dwarves collected their dead and laid them in an area together. The Rock titans, who had transported the dwarf battalion there, would first take the bodies back to their city.

"Will you be needin' a ride?" the dwarf asked her.

"We need to go to Orian Citadel to the south."

The dwarf thought for a moment. "We need to return to our king as soon as possible, but we owe ya. We will ensure your safety part of the way."

Ohn'na nodded her thanks. "Any help would be welcome. It would be a long trek without mounts or supplies."

"And when those orcs find out what happened to their mine, they aren't going to be too happy," Aden added.

A power in the north noted the silence in one of its territories. It briefly wondered if the chief there had finally found a way to dispose of the liaison that greatly irked him. However, Roxx's loyalty was unshakable, so the chances of that were slim.

To obtain another liaison would be of little effort, and it expected to get a report of what was happening from the chief soon. If it didn't, the wrath of its displeasure would be a sight to behold for the many puny mortals of this world.

25

ELWOOD

"We are all knights of the Avant Guard."

True to their word, the dwarves had asked the remaining titans to take the knights as far south as they could before dawn. The dwarves were anxious to get back to their king, but allowed the Rocks to shuttle them through the night.

Aden welcomed the time they had to rest. Frafnar lent him some extra clothing, and it was a relief to be warm and dry again. They were safe, so he easily fell into a deep, undisturbed sleep.

The knights took refuge in an underground chamber, created by the Rock titans. It moved solely by the will and power of the Rocks and was similar to the structure they'd used to forge their weapons. But instead of descending deeper into the ground they traveled through it. The only sound was the constant low rumble as they were carried through rock and soil. The rolling rhythm was a welcome reminder of the titans who accompanied them, a soothing comfort in their slumber. They reached the outskirts of the vast Elwood Forest just as the sun began to peek over the horizon. The knights awoke to the sudden silence and, since they were stationary, the lull of the rocking was gone.

"We go no further, dawn has come. We return to the west," the Rocks said as they opened the chamber and allowed the knights to leave the darkness and enter into the crisp morning air.

"Thank you for bringing us this far." Ohn'na bowed respectfully before the titans sank back into the ground.

Aden tried to stretch out his muscles, but everything hurt from the strain of the previous day. The recent inactivity had caused him to stiffen, and the slightest movement caused his body to complain. Frafnar took hold of his arm to help him stand and exit the chamber.

"You sound like an old man from all the noises you make." Freesha rolled her eyes. "You are not the only one who has seen battle recently. Do you hear us complain?"

"Let him be, he's a newly dubbed knight. In time he'll adjust to the rigors of duty, as we have." Ohn'na gave Aden a little sympathetic smile. "Work it out slowly, it'll get better. I'll find a remedy to ease the discomfort."

"Elwood?" Frafnar guessed after he'd scanned their surroundings, undoubtedly desperate to change the subject.

"Looks like it," Ohn'na agreed. "Orian Citadel will be just

to the south. It should take us a couple days to make it through the woods."

"Good thing the dwarves gave us some supplies." Even talking made Aden's body ache, but he was careful to quiet his complaints when Freesha narrowed her eyes at him.

They kept the pace slow for Aden's sake, but as time went on he walked easier. Ohn'na was able to find some bark from a particular tree that made his aches subside. Chewing it hadn't been too pleasant, but the relief it provided was welcoming.

The group easily navigated through the large trees before them. Elwood was a vast and ancient forest, rumored to have survived the ages, even from the times when the druid populations thrived. There were stories that roaming clusters of their people still protected the forest to this very day. Aden suspected that Ohn'na might know something about the truth to that. Her mother was a druid, after all, and there was an unmistakable anticipation in her eyes as they journeyed through the woods. If there were druids, Aden saw no sign of them, only flora that seemed to go on forever. Birds chirped in the trees, while squirrels foraged and chased each other. A light breeze played through the leaves, carrying the scent of soil and pollen. Any creatures that caught wind of the knights' passing stopped to stare, then returned to their business.

Aden was glad of the change of scenery. They'd spent too much time underground, in the dark, and among burning buildings and old ruins. The forest was teeming with life and activity, and he felt it refresh and uplift his spirits. It reminded him of the small garden he'd visited recently, but he didn't linger on the thought for too long, purposely distracting himself with the drama of the squirrels nearby.

They walked until the sun was at high time, then decided to take a break next to a small stream they'd been following south. The air had warmed considerably since the morning, making the group thankful for the shade of the trees and the cool relief of the breeze. Aden chewed on more of the bark after he sat, the effort still too much for his battered and bruised body. He took a swig from his waterskin and it revitalized him a bit.

"We should find a place to camp before nightfall." Freesha put her hands on her hips, as if giving an order.

Ohn'na tilted her head toward the sky. "We still have plenty of daylight left; there is some time before we need to look."

Freesha sent the guardian an incredulous look. "We don't know this area and shouldn't be caught in the open when night falls."

The two women obviously had a different approach, and the line of authority hadn't been established. Their goal to reach the citadel was clear, but who was in charge wasn't so obvious. Aden saw Frafnar sit back with an amused smirk and snack on his rations while he watched the two bicker.

Ohn'na turned to the others for their opinions. "What do you two think? As a group, perhaps it would be best if these decisions are made unanimously."

"Oh no," Frafnar shook his head, "you aren't dragging us into this one."

Freesha pointed, and Aden could almost hear the unspoken *ah-ha!* "You turn to them because you know I'm right."

"Oh, why don't you just turn into a bird and fly the rest of the way without us?"

Freesha scrunched her nose. "Change into one of those mindless beasts? Never."

"Oh, I don't know," Frafnar said, egging them on. "To be able to fly would be rather interesting."

Aden had wisely stayed out of the discussion until a noise caught his attention. A low snort caused the others to look in the direction of their visitor. A bear stood only a few feet away, eyeing the group cautiously. It reared back on its hind legs and roared a challenge.

"No one move," Ohn'na whispered.

Aden couldn't believe when Freesha rushed past him with her weapon drawn, and simply ignored Ohn'na's warning.

"It's only a bear."

Ohn'na tried to stop her, but it was too late. Freesha was already before the animal and swung her blade in a deadly arc.

"Stop!" A voice boomed and echoed, bursting with power. A man loomed on a large root nearby and slammed the end of his staff into it, and a loud crack of thunder followed.

Freesha's weapon was repelled by nothing but the air. The bear returned to its four paws and lumbered away unharmed.

"Var'rune... is that you?"

"You know him?" Aden's attention bounced from the guardian, to the man, and back again.

The stern set of Var'rune's face blossomed into one of joy. "Ohn'na?"

"She seems to know everyone," Freesha said and flung up her arms.

"What are you doing here?" Ohn'na asked, ignoring the gibe.

"I was tracking the bear and followed it here to find your overzealous friend attacking it."

"It was threatening us, so I acted in self-defense." Freesha squared her shoulders and matched his hard stare.

"Are you sure? Or *is it only a bear?*" Aden was glad he wasn't on the receiving end of Freesha's glare, but Var'rune merely returned his attention to Ohn'na. "Some of your friends have questionable character."

"We are all knights of the Avant Guard," Ohn'na replied. Aden saw the momentary glance to Freesha. "Sometimes we make mistakes and forget ourselves."

"Then the standards of the Order really have fallen."

Freesha's hands balled into fists. "Why you, arrogant, stubborn—" but she held back any further retorts and turned to Ohn'na. "Let's move on."

"*You* aren't going any further. You're fortunate I found you before any of the others; they would've attacked without question."

"Why would they do that?" Aden blurted.

Var'rune leaned on his staff. "Because of the tiv'veshier

you walk with. She may hide behind another form, but we know what she truly is."

Aden wasn't the only one baffled by the word. He saw the others look as puzzled as he was, with one exception.

Ohn'na lowered her gaze as she explained. "It means... goblin in the common tongue."

"That's impossible," Aden said. "The Order would never— This has to be some kind of mistake."

"I can assure you there's no doubt. She is tiv'veshier."

Aden looked at Ohn'na. "You knew?"

Her answer resounded through her silence, and it made him take a step back.

He turned to Frafnar. "Did you know about this?"

"What does it matter?"

Aden spun away from the others as he wrestled with the news, and he felt Ohn'na's eyes on his back.

"The rest of you may go, but she cannot. Only death awaits her any further," Var'rune continued.

"Then I enact the right of sorvynal'is: safe passage for one under my care."

Ohn'na's declaration made Aden spin around sharply, but he realized that Var'rune was as shocked as he was.

"They attack and kill our people! Yet you would still invoke the right for this tiv'veshier?"

"She's a knight of my Order, and the keepers trust her. So for her, yes." Ohn'na held her ground.

Var'rune appeared ready to argue, but he held those words back. "As is your right. You understand you take responsibility for her. You will bear the punishment of any transgressions?"

"I understand."

"This isn't necessary." Freesha frowned. "We can go around the forest, or I can go alone."

"No. We stay together."

"And that would take too long," Frafnar added.

Var'rune jumped down from his perch on the large root and handed Ohn'na two small pouches. "You know the markings. I'll let you apply them."

Freesha raised an eyebrow, but Frafnar spoke first. "I have orc blood in my veins; do I need this protection as well?"

The druid thought for a moment. "We share no love for the orcs, but they don't see you as one of their own. You are an oddity, and your behavior will be monitored. So no, if you stay with your companions you won't have a problem."

Ohn'na moved closer to Aden and spoke to him privately. "Are you all right with this?"

Aden found it hard to swallow, but he nodded. "As you say, she's part of the Order and was Khodi's mentor. And... you're willing to defend her. So, if you're certain, I trust your judgment."

The guardian put a comforting hand on his shoulder. "She isn't to blame for your pain, nor do I believe the Order would allow her to join if she was like her kin."

"I know. I just need... time."

Ohn'na gave him an encouraging pat when Var'rune's words grabbed their attention. "I will inform the others of your passing."

One moment Aden was looking at the man, then he

blinked, and where Var'rune had been, a cougar stood. Aden knew it was no ordinary animal.

Druids.

"Argh, this stuff stinks like nothing else. Is it done yet?" Freesha was attempting to scratch, but Ohn'na slapped her hand away to inspect it.

"It's dry, probably ready to come off."

While Freesha was busy washing her face in the nearby stream, Aden asked, "What is it?"

"A powder made from the leaves of a tree-shrub mixed with honey. The powder will temporarily stain the skin and the honey secures it. I put the markings of sorvynal'is on her face and hands. It symbolizes complete protection to all druids."

"What keeps anyone from just killing her?"

Aden thought Frafnar's question was a good one, certain that many people imagined doing so.

"Any druid wouldn't dare. If they did, then by druid law they would endure the same punishment as they'd used against the protected. Even if the person under sorvynal'is were to do wrong, their protector would bear the consequences, and the protected would then be driven from the area. Only if they returned would they be killed, if the offense justified that punishment."

"Just don't get caught." Frafnar shrugged.

Ohn'na shot Frafnar an incredulous stare, and then Aden

realized the implication of her decision. "So, you bear the responsibility now."

Ohn'na didn't comment, and Freesha returned from cleaning her face. The dry paste was now gone but the markings remained, stained into her skin. Var'rune returned then too, approaching from the shadows of the trees. "With my guidance, you will shave days off your journey through the forest. The others would like to meet Clar'rel's daughter again, so on our way south we should reach the gathering place by nightfall."

26

DRUIDS

"...it could go either way."

All were silent as they traveled, Var'rune leading them from the front. Ohn'na found her thoughts straying to her childhood memories, her life before leaving for the Order. Her eyes lingered on Var'rune's back as he walked ahead, but she tore her gaze away before the others took note. It had been a long time ago, and they only had a few brief encounters through the years. But even so, her eyes would return to him, feeling a childish nervousness and tightness in her gut. She forced her eyes away again for the final time.

Just as Var'rune had predicted, they reached their destination by sundown. The group discovered that the meeting place was a large glade in the forest. Even as they crossed the tree line, six smaller campfires blazed around the circular clearing while a seventh larger fire burned in the center. Fireflies danced in the dark places between the lights, and the moon was bright enough to reveal the others emerging from the woods. Ohn'na recognized them as her mother's people, some wearing light armor while others preferred plain clothing. Like Var'rune, a few of them chose to plant their staves in the ground, while the tops glowed with magic and enhanced the majestic sense of the place. Others brought pieces of wood from the forest and assembled tables, placing fruits, berries, and other treats on them. It wasn't long before meat roasted on the fires as well, and the smell wafted through the air. The knights were impressed with the effective community organization. All except for Freesha, who stood back with crossed arms and a persistent frown.

"So these are druids?" Aden asked.

No one ever saw these people, unless they wished to be seen. Various folklore spread throughout the lands about them, but Ohn'na knew them as any normal people. They walked with more grace, like their elf cousins, and the magic about them was unmistakable.

Ohn'na nodded. "They are the descendants of the druids of old."

As the people finished their work, they gathered to welcome the knights. Var'rune left to organize a watch of the perimeter to ensure the safety of everyone. He would join them when another took his place. Ohn'na couldn't hold back her small smile. Var'rune was still as dutiful as ever, ensuring the safety of their people came first, above all else.

She caught wind of the roasting meat, and her stomach

rumbled while her mouth watered. Rations had kept the hunger at bay, but she hadn't had a true meal since leaving Longshield Citadel. She suspected it was the same for the others, but it would be poor manners if the knights indulged themselves before they'd greeted their hosts. Fortunately, the druids were eager to meet them, and one such woman approached Ohn'na with a warm smile. By human standards she looked like she'd seen about thirty seasons, but the wisdom in her eyes couldn't hide the centuries she'd witnessed.

"Welcome back, daughter of Clar'rel."

Freesha kept to herself, and the druids seemed content with leaving her alone. None approached her, but many sneaked glances in her direction, bombarding her with a variety of expressions. As she had expected, most displayed fear or suspicion, and a few showed indisputable disgust. Others studied her with discreet curiosity, which was the most cordial reaction any of her kind could hope to receive. She ignored them all and centered her interest on sampling the food. She was in the middle of deciding what to try next when she sensed someone standing nearby, watching her with obvious intent. "What do you want?"

It was the druid woman who had greeted them earlier. "To talk. Our people rarely get to do so."

"There's nothing to say," she replied and plopped a berry in her mouth. It was more sour than she'd expected, and the taste made her cringe.

Despite Freesha's frosty disposition, the woman wouldn't be deterred so easily. "There's always something to say, beyond the threats and insults that usually dominate the dialogue between our people."

Freesha turned to the druid who'd intruded on her privacy. As she sized up the woman, she sensed her power. "You're... one of the old ones, aren't you?"

"I am Shana'oln Kirus, but you may call me Shana." She bowed in greeting. "And as old as you look in human years, you are young for your kind."

Freesha stiffened. She wasn't accustomed to anyone seeing through her facade. It unnerved her, but in the end her curiosity won over her discomfort. "Did you witness the war with the legendary dragons and demons?"

The woman formed a small, sad smile. "It was a long time ago, but yes, I remember."

After hiding for so long, it was strange speaking without reserve, but Freesha allowed herself to get lost in the moment. "What was it like? I've heard the tales, but I've wondered how your people..."

"It was terrifying," Shana replied, and Freesha was certain that she was being honest.

"Is it true your people would ride the dragons, wielding lightning through storm and wind, meeting your enemy in deadly combat?"

"Yes." The woman's face saddened. "Though it wasn't as glorious as you make it sound. Many died, and I hope this world never encounters such war again."

Freesha could only imagine the horror of it. There were

few who'd lived during those times; many of the druid people had been lost in the battles. Their populations had dropped dangerously low, and eventually the other races thrived while the druids retreated into the wilds to recover. Lost to history, they became legends. Their magic allowed them to change into the many animals in Mythreth, and some chose never to return to their true form.

The goblins had come to Mythreth during the war too, and competed for territory with the druids. Freesha didn't know if their populations would ever fully recover to the numbers they had long ago, especially from the constant attacks by her people. The goblins envied the druid power to change form by will alone. Goblin magic was restricted by having to consume the heart of any being before they achieved the ability to share the same form. Despite their disadvantage, the goblins managed to pressure the druids with their ferocity and persistence.

For Freesha, it all left a bad taste in her mouth. With the arrival of her people, the druids were being pushed further into extinction. In her mind, there was no need for any of it. It was a wide world with room for all. But her race was greedy, and their jealousy was boundless. Freesha admired this cluster of druids and how they interacted. She even felt a pang of envy, for the sense of community and trust the people here shared. If only her kin could learn to do the same.

"We've no words for trust, compassion, friendship, or love. My people value... other things," Freesha murmured, more to herself than to the woman who listened intently.

"Which is why you left them?" Shana inquired, and Freesha heard the slightest hint of hope in her tone.

She nodded slowly. "There were rumors that some groups felt differently, but I never found them. Perhaps lies made up to root out those like me. I would have been driven away or killed eventually, since I questioned too much."

"But you found someone who did?"

"Yes." That was all Freesha would share, and she said no more.

Shana nodded and pried no further. After a time, she spoke again. "There's someone I'd like you to meet. Please, come with me."

At first she was uneasy about the invitation, but Freesha remembered the markings, and the knowledge silenced her reservations. She followed the woman to one of the fires across the clearing. A boy in his adolescent years slept near the flames, but he still shivered despite his proximity to the heat. Even as cold as the boy appeared, he was soaked in sweat. He didn't stir as they approached, seemingly plagued by a deep and restless sleep. His breathing was shallow and labored, and at times he flinched from his dreams.

"He has a fever."

"Yes," Shana said. "His cluster was attacked by your kin. He was the only survivor, and has a venom in his veins that we cannot cure. Everything we've tried has slowed his decline, but I fear the poison will kill him soon."

Freesha turned to Shana for affirmation. "You'd ask me to try to save him? If he dies, your people will blame me."

"I wouldn't put this burden on you if there was another

choice. There *must* be something you know or could do to help him. You know your people better than anyone." Seeing Freesha was torn, the old druid tried again. "Please. If what you told me is true, you'd try to fix their wrongs. You are a knight of the Order, sworn to help those in need, and you are nothing like the tiv'veshier who revel in death and destruction. Please try, he's too young to be lost."

Freesha slowly rubbed her hands together. "There is one thing I know of that could work... but there is a danger. It may kill him."

Shana closed her eyes. "He'll die either way, but if there's even the slightest chance he'll live, do it. If you fear the consequences for you and your friends, I'll exonerate them from any blame." She cut the tip of her finger with her dagger and used the blood to trace an additional marking on Freesha's face."

"Why do you care so much?"

The woman paused. "He's my grandson." She finished her tracing and stepped back. "It's done."

Freesha's cynical side was mistrustful of the druid, wondering if the marking she'd placed on her meant anything at all. She ignored her suspicions and sensed the druid was indeed as desperate as she claimed.

"I have what my people call shaderoot. It only grows in certain areas but isn't greatly sought by my kin. To be poisoned by it alone isn't deadly, but it can be if a person is already weakened by another toxin. Fortunately, it has another very special property—it can counter other poisons. As I mentioned before, it could go either way."

"I understand." The woman struggled to remain in control, evident from the quiver in her words.

It took Freesha little time to ground the root into a powder and mix it with water. With the assistance of Shana, they slowly had the boy drink it. In either case, they would soon see a sign of the effects. The druid clasped her hands together and whispered words of prayer, while Freesha kept a close eye on the boy. It wasn't long before his breathing returned to normal and his shakes subsided. Color returned to his face and he slept peacefully. Freesha released a breath she hadn't realized she'd been holding.

Shana caught her in a hug and squeezed tight. "Thank you. Thank you—so much." Tears welled in her eyes as her words shook with emotion.

Freesha freed herself from the woman's embrace, and checked the boy again. Certain that the poison had sealed his fate, she stood in disbelief. "It will take some time for him to recover but... he's going to be fine."

A smile lit Shana's face, and the tears streamed down her cheeks. She hugged her again, but this time Freesha didn't tear herself away.

27

———————

SOIREE

"…it hasn't been easy."

———————————————————————

Somewhere in the camp, someone started to strum an instrument, and their voice rose through the air. The tune was slow, and the melody perfectly harmonized with the background chatter of the druids. Once Ohn'na had finished with the greetings, she rejoined Aden and Frafnar at their table. Aden saw her eyeing the large plump leg of some sort of cooked bird and nabbed it before he could swing his plate away.

"Hey!"

"Sorry, hungry," Ohn'na said through huge mouthfuls.

"Watch your fingers." Frafnar offered her a platter of her own. "You don't want to accidentally eat them too while you wolf that down."

"And there's a bone in that, don't choke on it." Aden chimed in.

"Ha. You guys are so funny." Ohn'na wiped her mouth and slowed her pace.

Despite his teasing, Aden sympathized with her. He for one was happy they didn't have to eat rations again. He savored the warm and fresh food and ate until he was full, since the druids had provided plenty for all.

"They don't normally do this. They mustn't have had a gathering for some time." Ohn'na's gaze pored over the crowd. "And speaking of gatherings, where's Freesha?"

"She joined one of the druids at their fire across the clearing." Aden motioned with his head in the direction she'd gone. "Hopefully making friends."

Ohn'na bit her lip. "If there's any trouble, I'll be the first to know about it."

"I think we jinxed it," Frafnar said when he spotted Var'rune approaching.

The man stopped a few paces away. "Ohn'na. I hadn't the chance to greet you before. I had a few things to attend to, you understand."

Aden noted that he wasn't the only one to release the breath he held, and their relief remained a mystery to their visitor.

Var'rune hesitated. "I... hope I'm not interrupting anything."

"Ah, no!" Ohn'na said a little too quickly. "Not at all, please join us."

Var'rune cleared his throat. His arms were clasped behind

his back, and he subtly shifted his weight from one foot to the other. Aden's gaze drifted from Var'rune to Ohn'na. He did his best to hide his grin and elbowed Frafnar beside him, who was draining the contents of his cup when the unexpected jab caused him to spray his drink. Once Aden had Frafnar's attention he tilted his head in the direction of another fire.

"Please excuse us." Aden bowed slightly then headed toward another nearby fire with Frafnar at his heels, who decided to tease him once they were out of earshot.

"You know, if you wanted to get me alone, you just had to ask."

His face must have portrayed exactly what Frafnar was aiming for because his friend's pretense of seriousness crumbled into laughter.

"That's not funny."

"That look was pretty funny."

Aden punched his friend firmly on the side of his arm, and Frafnar only grinned more.

Ohn'na was conversing with Var'rune when she saw a woman appear from behind him. Her raven hair was tied into a side braid that fell over her shoulder and ended at her waist. She was tall and stood with an air of arrogance.

"Well, well. So this must be the daughter of Clar'rel everyone's talking about."

"Vix'an, you are supposed to be at your post," Var'rune said, unable to hide the annoyance in his voice.

"And miss meeting this wonder of the world? I've never had the pleasure." She curtsied in a bow full of mockery. "I am Vix'an Tardol. It's an honor to be graced with your presence." She continued on without waiting for a response from Ohn'na. "It's not every day I can meet the mix-blood prodigal daughter." Her every word was venom embellished with pleasantries.

"The pleasure is mine." Ohn'na managed to get out while the woman took a breath. Ohn'na couldn't understand why she was the focus of such loathing, since she'd never met the druid before. Each time Vix'an laid her eyes on Var'rune, Ohn'na thought she saw adoration in them, and her insight was quickly verified.

"Do you know that our family lines do not cross at any point in history? We are the perfect pair." Vix'an then made a pouting face that didn't hold a smidgen of sincerity. "Aw, too bad you left for your Order. He and I will now lead our people."

"I haven't accepted your proposal," Var'rune said, and his eyes narrowed.

"You haven't rejected it either." She looked at Ohn'na as she said it, like she hoped the words stung.

"I have, in fact, every time."

Vix'an snorted and shrugged. "You'll change your mind once you realize I am the best choice. And when the nights get cold and lonely."

Ohn'na stiffened at the thought, and it was obvious Var'rune was about to lose his patience. Fortunately, Aden and Frafnar spotted the disruptive druid and swooped in to help. They each tucked one of her arms in theirs and led her away.

"I hear you are the best dancer of the druids." Aden waved a hand in a wide swing.

"Yes," Frafnar chimed in, "you must show us; we'd love to see it."

Vix'an pulled away at first, but the compliments were successful at appealing to her vanity. "Well... all right." A broad grin spread on her smug face. "I am the best, after all. It would be a crime not to indulge adoring admirers."

Ohn'na caught Frafnar rolling his eyes, and Aden gave her a quick wink.

"You have good friends there."

Var'rune's words made her smile. "I do."

"I'm sorry for that. Ever since she joined us from another cluster, she hasn't left me alone."

"It seems you have your hands full these days." Ohn'na pitied him, knowing all the challenges that could arise with his position.

"Since your mother left, it hasn't been easy."

Ohn'na knew there was no judgment or resentment in his words, but the guilt still weighed on her. Clar'rel had left soon after Ohn'na joined the Avant Guard. Her mother had chosen to travel the world with her father, leaving the responsibility of her people to others. Var'rune had grown up to take on that role, his natural leadership qualities benefiting their cluster. It hadn't taken much to convince them that he was right for the role.

In truth, the duty should have been Ohn'na's, but her life

in the Order had prevented her from fulfilling it. She would sometimes imagine what her life would have been like if she'd stayed with the druids, but the good the Order did for all kingdoms seemed more important. Her people had Var'rune now to lead them, which made her feel more at peace with her decision. She still regretted the hardships her friend endured, from a duty he was not meant to bear. He rose to the challenge, though, and thrived, well suited to lead and protect their people. "I guess my mother hasn't visited for some time?"

Var'rune took a seat next to her, resting against the edge of the table. "Not since the last snowmelt, months ago."

"I see." When they'd encountered him earlier, Ohn'na had hoped her parents would still be here. But unfortunately, it was not meant to be.

"Don't trouble yourself about any of this," he assured her. "We get by just fine."

Ohn'na became very aware of his proximity now. She tried not to stare, absorbing all she could in the short time she allowed herself to look at him. He'd grown much since his adolescent years. His shoulders had broadened out, and his jaw was lined with short stubble. He wore a plain vest, which couldn't hide the firm muscles beneath. His hair remained the same, resting at a length that covered his ears but didn't touch his shoulders. The color had darkened to a deep brown since childhood. His dark eyes seemed to study her with interest.

Ohn'na felt very self-conscious all of a sudden. What he must think of her as she appeared, dirty and disheveled. She briefly wondered how she now compared to her younger self and if he noticed any differences. She tried to keep her hands steady as she tucked a stray lock of hair behind her ear.

"It has been some time since we last talked," Var'rune said softly.

"It has."

Ohn'na heard the tempo of the music increase, and some drums, flutes, and other instruments join in. Var'rune took her hand, and Ohn'na felt excitement rush through her like electricity.

"Would you dance with me? Like we used to?" The hope in his eyes was so fragile, like she could crush his spirit with but a word.

Ohn'na was breathless, and for an instant forgot her words but managed to nod. Her heart warmed at his smile, and he led her to dance among the crowd who were already moving in rhythm with the music.

Aden and Frafnar watched as more druids joined in to dance. Fortunately, after realizing neither the guests nor Var'rune were paying attention to her, Vix'an had stomped off.

"Ohn'na is having fun," Aden said, glad that the intrusive druid woman hadn't ruined the evening for his friend.

They continued to take in the dancing from the side. Frafnar nudged him after a time, pointing out the woman they had saved Ohn'na from earlier. Apparently she was trying very hard to get one man to dance with her. When that failed, she spotted them and headed in their direction.

"Look busy!" Aden whispered, but it was already too late.

"Say, you wouldn't care for a dance, would you?" Vix'an spoke to Aden with large eyes and pouty lips.

"Uh, no thanks."

She must have realized Frafnar was her last hope; she tactfully wrapped an arm around his shoulders. "How about you? You aren't a sourpuss like your friend, are you? I promise we'll have a good time."

Frafnar returned her smile. Her delight ended abruptly, though, when he grabbed her hand and threw it off of him, as one might do with a bug. His grin remained.

"You fools." She cursed as she once again stormed off.

"I almost pity her." Aden said when the woman was gone. "She just has a high opinion of herself, and wants to be adored."

"More like worshipped." Frafnar shook his head. "She should get off her high horse."

They continued to watch the dancing until two women approached them. "Excuse us, but we were just wondering if you two were..." She looked at her companion for help, but the other woman merely shrugged. At a loss for the word, the druid pressed her two index fingers together.

Her meaning dawned on Aden. "What? No—why would you think that?"

"You both have the same scent..."

Aden wasn't sure how they knew, but he looked down at himself and remembered he was wearing Frafnar's clothing. "We... no! I... my clothes were wet and I borrowed his."

"You sound offended. Am I not good enough for you?"

Frafnar put his hand to his heart and feigned being wounded. "What, am I not handsome enough?"

"Not helping!"

Frafnar laughed then turned his attention back to the women. "Why do you ask?"

"Well, if you are able, we'd like to dance."

"We'd be honored." Frafnar took a little bow then motioned for the ladies to lead the way.

Aden lightly hit his friend's arm. "*Not* funny."

"Come on, life can't always be doom and gloom. And this is a party; have some fun for a change." Frafnar winked and then followed the druids to join in the merriment.

Aden sighed. He was glad his friend was able to relax and enjoy the festivities. While he followed, he briefly wondered what orc celebrations were like, but it soon slipped his mind as he lost himself to the rhythm of the music.

"I... could go with you."

The *dwarves have returned safe."* Nannelle heard the voice of a knight reporting through the exten stone. *"There were some casualties, but the burials have been arranged and the families notified. The dwarves who returned said that the knights were unharmed and are headed back south to Orian Citadel."*

When Ohn'na had reported the situation, Nannelle had sent a message to a knight in the vicinity of the High Peaks to the north. Fortunately, the dwarven King Balendur, in his wisdom, had kept the gift of the exten stone the Order had given them long ago. Its value was unknown to the dwarves, since it only appeared as an ordinary stone. It now allowed the knight she'd sent to report back.

Unlike the exten stones, verge stones were commonly used to communicate between members of the Order. They were light and small enough to easily carry, but the amplification range was limited. The stones received messages sent by the more powerful stones, but weren't capable of sending anything over great distances. Knights in the field used them to relay messages to other members of the Order, if they were within range.

In special circumstances, some knights would shoulder the burden of carrying aphix stones, such as Ohn'na had done to ensure she was able to inform the keepers about the situation. Aphix stones were generally used within the citadels, their large size and greater mass making them difficult to carry. Most preferred to use the verge stones, while the aphix stones remained stationary in the rooms and quarters of the citadels.

Since the attack on Orian Citadel, and the increased number of murders and disappearances of their members, the magisters thought it prudent to establish new protocols. Knights were now required to wear newly designed verge stones, flat and polished to be easily worn as a pendant, hidden beneath clothing. The constant contact with the stone would help knights to work together more efficiently and allow messages from the keepers to be received promptly. Research to broaden the range of the verge stones was ongoing, but so far it didn't look promising. The stones were also now engraved with the owner's name and rank, for ease of identification, organization, and recognition. Keepers were no exception to these new protocols. Nannelle barely felt the weight of the pendant around her neck. The new design was impressive.

"The king sends his gratitude for the part our Order played in freeing his people from the orcs," the knight continued, distracting Nannelle from her thoughts. *"And he hopes you'll allow Amell Thach to return as soon as possible to continue her work."*

Nannelle's eyebrows rose. *"Even in the midst of the war declaration by the orcs?"*

"It seems especially so," the knight replied. *"He appears to be confident that they can repel their attacks, though I feel he's holding some information back. The orcs are resistant to magic, so the motivation for continuing the research is unclear. What is so important that he would risk war? He'll continue to send his people into the orc territories, even amid the hostilities it will cause."*

Nannelle wished she could speak to the king directly, but since he hadn't the gift, the exten stone was just any other rock to him. Amell would return to her people, and Nannelle would speak to the king. *"Inform King Balendur that I will personally escort his researcher home."*

"Keeper, if I may. Is that really wise? The people here seem wary even in my presence. Some are even hostile. If I weren't under the king's protection—"

"I appreciate your concern, but it's unnecessary. You may return to your previous mission once you inform the king of my message. Thank you for your service."

There was a pause before the knight replied. *"It was my honor, Keeper. Please be safe."*

"Be safe." The connection ended, and Nannelle lifted her

hand from the exten stone as the warm glow from it faded until it once again looked like any ordinary large rock.

"That was amazin'," Amell said after observing the change of the stone. "I've seen Ohn'na use magic, but she has druid blood in her veins. I never thought I'd see one of our own people usin' it." She looked back at the stone and studied it. "You say you can communicate with other knights usin' these? I didn't hear you say a word!"

Nannelle nodded. "We can project our thoughts so others can hear them. The stones amplify our powers to extend the distance we can connect with our peers, who are also using stones. There are different types we use."

"Ohn'na has shown me her verge stone, and also the aphix stone, but I've never seen one as large as this." Amell moved to the center of the room where a rock the size of a small boulder lay. Half of it was cradled in a basin of marble that extended out to border the round shape. The edge was wide enough for a place to sit and provide comfort for those long conversations.

"That is the amass stone, and the only one of its kind in this citadel. There is one in every citadel of the Order, and this is how the Councils communicate across the lands."

"And the one you just used is an exten stone?"

"Yes. We use these to send out messages to knights in the field. The larger the stone, the greater the distance it can be used to communicate."

"I see," Amell said. "And only members of your Order can use them? What about other mages?"

Nannelle shook her head. "Only people with true gritt."

Amell put her hand against the amass stone, but nothing

happened. Nannelle couldn't imagine her life without magic. To hear someone's thoughts from afar was useful. Throughout her life she'd wondered what it would have been like to live among her people. There were many times she'd wished to visit the dwarves, and now here was an opportunity to do so.

"We'd better prepare for the journey to High Peaks."

"Yes," Amell said and dropped her hand from the stone. "My people are goin' to get a shock when they meet a dwarf who has power as you do."

"Let's hope the reception is welcoming."

The group of knights finally emerged on the other side of Elwood after the journey had taken a few more days than expected. Aden suspected that was no accident. He knew the others had noticed it too, but no one said a word. Freesha especially had been surprisingly quiet. Perhaps she saw how much this time meant to Ohn'na, and decided a day or two more wouldn't make a difference.

The group could view the citadel from their position, just beyond the tree line. The last time they'd seen it, it had been on fire. Smoke no longer rose from the structure, and other than the scorch marks and rubble it looked peaceful once again. Ohn'na was saying her goodbyes to Var'rune some distance away down along the edge of the forest, while the others gave them the privacy they needed.

"I think she's forgotten we exist." Frafnar smirked.

Of course, Aden knew he was talking about Ohn'na, and

how she hadn't left Var'rune's side during the entire journey. It was obvious that a relationship had blossomed between the two, revealing their long-suppressed feelings. Aden was happy for her.

"I'm surprised she doesn't stay with him," Freesha blurted out. "Isn't that what people do if they care for each other? They should want to be together."

"She'd never abandon her duty; her work is too important."

"I'm sure she's considered it." Freesha shrugged. "As many do when thinking of having families."

"They only just started their relationship, I doubt she is thinking about that already." Frafnar argued.

Aden chuckled. "In any case, let's not ruin this for her and give them some space."

Ohn'na glanced in the group's direction. They chatted among themselves, giving her the courtesy of privacy as they directed their attention to the citadel in the distance. "They are waiting for me."

"I... could go with you. I never told you how much I regretted letting you leave alone when you joined your Order..."

Ohn'na shook her head, smiling. "You know as well as I that you can't. You are responsible for our people, and they need you. Keep them safe, and tell my parents of me when they visit."

Var'rune returned her smile. "Your mother will ensure I

don't forget. She and your father always ask about you." He then took her hand in his and kissed it. "Please be careful, I want to see you again."

"You will." She touched the verge stone that now hung at his neck, fastened with twine. "When I can visit, I'll call."

"Even if you can't, please let me know how you are. Even if my messages can't reach you, know I'll always be here if you need me."

She'd known he was also gifted with willful magic, but when she'd joined the Order, he'd stayed behind to look after their people. It was as if their paths were destined to go in different directions, but she vowed that they would cross more often.

"It's a promise." She embraced him one last time, then tore herself away to join her friends. If she stayed any longer she might never leave. Halfway across the distance she succumbed to the need to look back. A large stag stood where Var'rune had been, never taking his eyes from her.

Ohn'na returned to the group. "Sorry for the delay. Let's get back to the citadel and resume our duties." Surprisingly, the others didn't say much as they began the last leg of the journey. She was grateful, though, as she didn't feel like answering the awkward questions they were probably thinking.

"I love you."

The words whispered in her mind suddenly, like they had been carried on the wind. She turned to look back at the tree line, but Var'rune was gone. She took the aphix stone out of her pocket that she'd been holding from the moment they'd parted. She opened her fingers and admired it warmly, as if it had been the source of his affections.

"Everything all right?" Aden paused to call back to Ohn'na, who'd fallen behind.

She returned the stone to her pocket and joined her companions. "Yes, everything is wonderful," she replied, and a new smile spread across her face.

A figure clutched his head as the pain reminded him of his humiliation. *Where are you? Where are you! Sooner or later you'll have to return to the citadel...*

His misery was nothing compared to what he had in store for her. He would show her the meaning of true agony. First, her precious trainee. Then the Order.

"I look forward to seeing the look on your face as I kill those you care about." Laughter filled the air. "Soon, Ohn'na Sazi. Very, very soon..."

There was a knock on the door, and the Slaver entered the room.

The figure straightened and spun to face him. "I have a job for you."

29

SET IN MOTION

"...it's only going to get worse before it gets better."

"What do you mean this isn't enough evidence?" Amell's frustrations rang in her every word. "She's livin', breathin' proof that dwarves once worked with magic, once had magic. What else would the people need?"

"You'll address his highness with more respect!" the king's general ordered.

"Relax, Redarin, there's no need for formalities here." King Balendur motioned for the man to take his seat.

General Redarin composed himself and did as he was bid. His eyes never left Amell, though. Amell matched the general's stare with her own unwavering determination. In the short time since Nannelle had met the woman, she knew Amell would say what needed to be said, and how it needed to be said, king or not. A smokeless fire burned in the circular indent in the center of the stone table. The flames were cold compared to the heated looks shared between Amell and the general.

"Some would argue that today, any magic our people possess is from the mix of bloodlines with other races, not from the origins of our ancestors," the king continued. "The people won't be swayed until we can link our past directly with magic."

"We may be doomed never to find it." Redarin spoke of a very realistic possibility.

King Balendur folded his hands on the table before him. "We must. We blamed magic for drivin' us below ground. To move forward, we have to put our doubts aside and recognize that it's a force to acknowledge. To do this, we need to continue excavatin' the old ruins, even if they are now within the orc territories."

Keeper Nannelle sat back in her chair and wondered why Balendur was so determined. She decided it would be best if she remained silent throughout the meeting, though, as her presence was the only thing Amell had required, and not a testimony. She already knew of the mistrust the dwarves held for magic, and she would welcome the change if they were to embrace it. The Avant Guard would then have easier dealings with them, and the dwarves with arcane abilities could live among their own people without fear. She wanted them to accept magic, but not at the expense of war and lives. It was unfortunate that the dwarves' covert operation hadn't gone undetected.

Amell frowned and Balendur continued. "I'm sorry. We tried it your way, but now we're committed to confront the orcs. They've called us to war and give us no choice. I know you worry about your sons, as would I. They can be assigned to safer duties, if that would help put your mind at ease."

Amell was about to answer when there was a knock on the thick wooden door. It swung open without invitation, and an armored dwarf marched in with her helm tucked under her arm. The young woman had her father's eyes, the same lively deep emeralds filled with pride and intelligence. Her short raven hair had a natural wave to it and was cropped just above her shoulders.

"Sorry, Your Majesty," one of the guards poked his head inside, "but she insisted."

The guard retreated from the room when the king waved him off and said to Nannelle, "This is my daughter, Maven."

"Welcome to our halls." The woman took a bow, and when she straightened, her face brightened at the sight of Amell's presence. "I'm glad you made it back safe. I'd heard the trouble you ran into with the orcs. I would've come liberate you myself but, well, you know how it is." She pointedly glanced at her father.

Nannelle heard the laugh, even as Amell attempted to mask it with a sudden cough. From what she could gather, Amell knew well the stress of parenthood, explaining how her own sons complained at times of her worry for them. Amell had also helped Maven see the king's side of things, and often spoke fondly of her.

"Father." Maven returned her attention to the king. "The

evacuation of the surface settlements is goin' as smooth as possible. It will take longer than expected to get everyone below ground, so I suggest we station more soldiers there to help reduce casualties if the orcs arrive before we're ready."

"Very well," Balendur said. "Anythin' else?"

"There are some who refuse to leave their homes. We are tryin' to persuade them to either join the fight or leave with everyone else, and not needlessly throw their lives away. Those who still won't budge we are arrestin' for their own good. They'll be able to return to their homes once this has been settled."

"What's the status on the relocation areas?" General Redarin asked.

"The technicians informed me that some of the space was already used to house our growin' population and may not have the ability to accommodate everyone. In this case, it might be prudent to ask families to house any friends or relatives who come in from the surface. Volunteers would also be welcome to take in some, and if there's still a problem, we should make it mandatory. The work in those areas was never finished, and the technicians are also workin' to get water and other necessities set up."

"Will we be able to keep so many?" Amell's eyebrows rose. "What about food, for the people, and the soldiers?"

"Those from the surface are bringin' what they can, and we've the means to grow some here, but if this war goes on too long we might run into a shortage. We can prolong the supplies by havin' everyone on half rations."

Nannelle wondered how their ancestors survived so long

below ground without food and supplies from the surface. "I believe the Avant Guard could provide aid in that endeavor, provided your people would accept such help."

King Balendur rubbed his chin. "Our people are startin' to slowly build our roots on the surface again. If they don't want to be driven back into the depths, they'll take whatever help is offered."

"Would your Order help in the battles?" General Redarin asked.

"That isn't for me to decide. I'll inform our leaders of your situation and appeal for aid."

"As it stands, our first priority is gettin' our people to safety. After that, we will continue this meetin' and decide how to proceed with the war and the excavations into the old ruins." King Balendur's tone was a definite dismissal, but as everyone started to leave, Nannelle spoke.

"Could I have a word, Your Majesty?"

Balendur motioned her forward. Once everyone had left and the great wooden door was shut behind them, Nannelle felt it time to speak her mind. "I can understand your desire to bring magic back to your people, but is it worth the lives this war will claim?"

"You understand?" the King asked with raised eyebrows.

"I sensed her gifts even as she entered the room."

Balendur sighed deeply and retook his seat. He clasped his hands before him and bent his head. "Nothin' gets past the Order, I see—true to your reputation." After a moment, he looked up. "Do you have children, Keeper?"

"No." None of her blood, but she viewed all trainees as her

children of sorts. It was the keepers' responsibility to ensure their safety while inside the citadel. She took it seriously, but from her many years of experience she knew the duty required more than to fill a role as mere protector and overseer. They were the heart of the Order.

"I'd do anythin' for my daughter. She's my only child and is the next in line to the throne." The king's hands tightened. "If the people were to know of her gifts..." His eyes focused on Nannelle once more. "That's why this is so important, but it's not only about her birthright. This world will once again be ruled by magic. As a people, we cannot afford to fall behind. Maven will lead them into the future, will *give* them a future."

Nannelle sat in the chair next to the king and put her hands on his, and she felt him relax from her act of tenderness. "I understand. You don't need to convince me, these are your people, but the reason for your decision will be useful when I represent your cause to the magisters. As unfortunate as war may be, it may be the only way to move forward. I can sympathize with your position." She gave him a little smile and hoped it gave him some encouragement.

"It's never easy." Balendur sighed heavily once again.

"And it's only going to get worse before it gets better."

It had been a week since Frafnar had returned to the citadel, but he rarely got to see Aden, who'd been tasked to help with repairs. Frafnar had just returned from a mission of his own that had taken a few days, but was now set on visiting Aden, no matter how busy either one was. He had to talk to him; he couldn't put it off any longer. Tomorrow would be too late. He'd be gone, and he couldn't leave without saying... something.

Frafnar finally neared the door to his friend's quarters but arrived at the same time as a messenger.

The woman looked at the door, then at him with obvious confusion. "Excuse me, but is this not Aden Fendrie's chambers? The citadel records are still a mess, and he's changed locations so many times—"

Frafnar held up a hand to silence further explanations. "Yes, what's this about?"

She twirled the scroll in her fingers. "He's to make this his top priority. We received an urgent request for aid from a small village in the vicinity of his upcoming venture."

"Why not send someone who's in the area? Isn't he doing enough already?"

"I wasn't briefed on the nature of the message, but the Order has few resources in that region. I assume Knight Fendrie is to negotiate this issue. He didn't answer any of our calls, so I was sent to give him the information in person."

Frafnar smiled to himself. *Knight Fendrie.* Since they'd arrived at the citadel their promotions had been made official, and they now enjoyed the freedoms of knighthood. To be addressed as such was an honor, something he'd never tire of hearing. Eventually, knights were expected to take on trainees of their own, but all Frafnar wanted was to be alone or go on assignments with those he trusted most.

It felt strange being back in the Order, not having to

constantly retaliate against schemes devised for him. His smile then slowly diminished. Because of his heritage, many still regarded him with a measure of suspicion, even in the Order. With the war coming against the dwarves, it would only get worse. When the magisters had agreed to send help, he decided that he'd volunteer to go. The dwarves' view of him may not be any better, but with his knowledge of orc tactics, he believed he could be of great benefit to the war. Plus, they still had a lot to answer for, and that alone would've fueled his motivations.

The urgent tapping of the messenger's foot warned him of the woman's impatience. Frafnar held out his hand. "I need to speak to him. I'll give Aden the information."

"As you wish." The woman tossed him the scroll and hurried off.

Frafnar faced the door, closed his eyes, and took a breath as he knocked. When there was no answer, he checked the handle. It was unlocked, so he stepped into the room. He found his friend slumped at his desk, sleeping soundly. He shook Aden's shoulder, and as he woke and rubbed his tired eyes, Frafnar spoke.

"The keepers really have you working hard." He looked around, noticing the state of the room, the chaos confirming the truth of it.

"Fraf? You're back?"

Frafnar handed Aden the scroll. "I intercepted this for you. It's supposedly your top priority."

Aden unrolled the parchment. "All right. It's bad enough

they want me on repair duty, but now they have me going on missions on top of it."

"Once the citadel is back to normal, things will slow for us again, and we'll be missing the busy days."

"I for one will not miss it for a long, long time." Aden's wry smile dropped when an object on Frafnar's belt caught his attention. "You still have the mask?"

"Habit."

After a moment's pause, Aden spoke again, but more as a statement than a question. "You're thinking of helping in the war, aren't you?"

Frafnar hesitated, but there was no denying it. "Yes."

Aden studied him. "You never told me why you despise the crimsons... you want to talk about it?"

"No."

Aden merely leaned back in his seat. Silence fell between them, but Frafnar was surprised to find understanding in his eyes.

"Will Freesha be going with you?"

"She wants to leave this place. She says there are too many painful memories here."

"I can empathize with that." Aden still avoided the gardens, where Khodi had died. "I'm glad someone will be covering your back out there. I'm almost tempted to join you, or ask you to stay. It might sound a little strange, but I'm going to miss our adventures."

Me too. A lump formed in his throat, and Frafnar coughed to clear it. "At least Ohn'na will still be around.... Excuse me, I just returned and came straight here. I'd better go get cleaned up."

He turned to leave the room but caught a glimpse of the smile that spread on Aden's face. He was one of the few Frafnar considered a friend, and as much as he needed to go, a large part of him wanted to stay. It was going to be harder to leave than he'd thought.

30

"The Order has become weak."

The next day, Frafnar and Freesha were on their way to the upper stables when they ran into Ohn'na. An unusual look of concern creased her face. "Ohn'na!" Frafnar called, but needed to wave his hands to get her attention. "What's wrong?"

"Oh! I'm glad I found you, I was looking all over for you!"

While Ohn'na caught her breath, Frafnar thought, *Wasn't I the one who found you?* Her next words made all humor escape his mind.

"Something's happened with Aden. He never made it to the negotiations yesterday, and we've received a message this morning. It threatens Aden's life unless I go meet the abductors. They named me specifically, but I don't know why."

Frafnar's mind raced. "What? How did this happen? Who would do this? What—?" He paused. Hadn't Aden been given a mission yesterday? A problem Aden was supposed to deal with before going to the negotiations? Hadn't he been the one to give it to him? "Why are you *still* here?"

Ohn'na took a step back from his sudden outburst. "I was on my way. Though the keepers don't approve of me going at this time"—she held up a hand to stop Frafnar's protests—"but have agreed if someone can teach the new recruits in my place. I've made up my mind, and they know I'm going, no matter what."

Frafnar wanted to yell in frustration but pointed a thumb at Freesha instead. "She'll do it. I'm going with you."

"Oh? Volunteering me for menial tasks now, are you...?"

But Frafnar barely heard her as he dashed down the hall with Ohn'na. "Thanks for getting me!"

"Of course! I had a feeling you'd want to come."

As usual, she'd been right.

Everything was still and silent, other than the swaying of fabric in the breeze. Aden dared not move. He was forced to stand at the edge of the ruins on the plateau, hundreds of feet above the treetops below. A nearby mountain rose above them, where a waterfall rushed to meet the rapids below. Aden stole a glance behind him and hoped he'd never have to experience the ground rushing to meet him. The air at this altitude was surprisingly warm, and it tugged at his hair and clothing. But if he wasn't careful, the wind could push him off with one sudden strong gust.

The ruins were nothing but a large rectangular slab of cracked stone atop a plateau. Large columns still bordered the edges, almost posing as markers where the floor suddenly ended and the walls no longer stood. The only entrance was the stone staircase that led up to the structure. Aden considered it had once served as a place where someone of authority received audience or enacted justice. Given his current situation, maybe he wasn't far off the mark.

His abductor stood at the base of a slab that was so worn that it could have once served as a seat, but was unrecognizable now. Ohn'na and Frafnar were near the stairs.

The knights pulled back the hoods of their cloaks as they were flanked by other figures, cutting off any hope of retreat.

"I'm surprised you expected us to try and run." Frafnar broke the silence. "Even more so that you found others to fight for your cause so quickly."

"Many hate the Avant Guard." Aden's captor smirked. "Once I have dealt with you, my army will grow once again."

Ohn'na took a step back. "It... can't be."

"Have you finally figured it out? Will my face remove any doubt you have?"

The man slid back his hood, and Ohn'na stared. "Garret Raismus."

Frafnar voiced Aden's own thoughts. "The son of Knight Servol Raismus?"

"Master Raismus now." The man glared, and the red of his irises stood out against the black of his eyes.

"Your father thought you were dead. He blamed the Council—"

"As well he should have! The keepers failed to rescue me, and my father was the only one who did what had to be done." His hands then clenched into fists. "And then you killed him."

Ohn'na didn't respond to that, but Aden recognized the pain in her eyes.

"Why didn't you come back?"

"The fools who captured me only succeeded with the help of another, a slaver who specialized in the capture of Avant Guard knights, mages, and others that would sell for a good price. They have contrived a way to disrupt magic, which prevented me from calling for help. They faked my death, taking the gold and their new slave. Everyone believed I was dead."

Sweat slid slowly down Aden's temple. *This isn't good. If Garret's revealing everything, he must be confident we'll be dead soon.* Aden looked around warily. Was that a shift in the air? Did some of the shadows move?

Directing his words to Ohn'na, Garret continued. "I did return. Fortunately for me, my captor made a mistake and I killed him. By that time, I'd been brought far from any outpost. I headed to the nearest citadel. During one of my stays in a tavern, I ran into a knight who knew my father and me and gave his condolences for Raismus's death. After I got rid of his corpse, I contacted the Order. The messengers aren't highly gifted, you see, and I was able to take control of her mind. Through her, I established a spy network and attained a representative for my goals."

The renegade leader, Aden thought, and Ohn'na appeared to share his surprise.

"You made her the leader, and controlled her mind from afar. Someone to take the fall for you if we retaliated."

Garret only laughed. "There are always weak-minded fools around to control."

"It was you from the very beginning."

Aden could see all the pieces falling into place. The unrest in the Order as knights were murdered and went missing. Guardian Cormell's death, and the sudden request for Ohn'na to guide a trainee. Garret had worked hard, pushing the Order into asking their available knights to become mentors. All to fulfill his ultimate desire to deeply hurt her. Then there was the artifact that Frafnar had found and given to the renegade leader, the messenger who'd been one of the first to disappear. The subsequent attack on newly established Orian Citadel, and the artifact, used in the battle to build an undead army against them. Garret hadn't anticipated the resilience and tenacity of the knights, resulting in the destruction of the relic and the death of his main pawn. Now his troops were defeated, scattered, or captured, which had forced Garret to finally reveal himself and enact his personal revenge against Ohn'na. Aden suspected that once Garret was done with her, he'd rebuild his army again to destroy the Order.

"Was it all worth it?" Ohn'na asked. "Has all this death and destruction been worth it? Your father loved you, and he died for his revenge. Don't make the same mistake. The Order does what it can, but it's not perfect."

"My father was right!" Garret gritted his teeth. "The

Order has become weak. They couldn't save me, as they cannot, and will not, save your trainee. You'll see the truth as I do, before you die."

A handful of figures materialized from nowhere—as the mirage spell around them fell away—and surrounded the knights. Aden's eyes went wide. *Crimsons!*

"Is this what you have been reduced to?" Frafnar yelled. "Relying on these suckling mercenaries?"

"The arrangement has been most beneficial for both sides. I get my revenge on Ohn'na and kill her kit, while they get to dispose of the mix-blood responsible for the destruction of their mine. You should feel honored: not many irk them as you do."

Aden had also been part of that debacle, but wisely let it slide.

Garret cleared his throat. "Now back to the business at hand. Give them your weapons, or I kill the prisoner."

"Don't do it!" Aden shouted. "He'll do it anyway, and then you'll—" Aden felt a conjured rope slither around his neck, like invisible fingers sliding around his throat. He felt his feet leave the ground and saw them dangle over the edge of the long drop. His hands were bound before him, so he was able to grab at the rope and take some of the pressure off his neck. Despite that, he still struggled to fill his lungs with air.

"Silence!" Garret's glare swung between the knights and his captive. He kept Aden suspended over the ledge.

If the knights attacked him now, the rope would disappear and he'd fall. Understanding this, they reluctantly dropped their weapons. The orcs grabbed Frafnar roughly and held him in place.

Ohn'na was well guarded, with blades pointed only inches from her. "Stop this, Garret! Don't follow the path of your father."

"Or what?" Garret's eyes cut into hers. "You'll kill me? Just like you killed him?"

Ohn'na bowed her head. Aden knew there had been little choice with Raismus, and now history might be about to repeat itself with his son.

"Now then." Garret's grin held no warmth. "I believe my allies would enjoy seeing their mix-blood die first. As eager as I am to see Ohn'na suffer as she loses her kit, I don't mind killing her old friend." He fingered the sword in one hand, bringing the flat of the weapon close to his face and looking at them past the steel. It was Aden's blade. "I wonder how it'll feel knowing you'll be cut down by your friend's weapon. If you resist, your friend dies in your place." He then used his powers to magnify his throw of the sword, sending it like a spear toward his victim.

The world slowed for Aden once again. His eyes followed the weapon as it spun on its axis toward its mark. Frafnar's expression was of steadfast resolve. *Just like Cormell.* The memory flashed in Aden's mind, and he saw his old guardian standing there and the dagger that flashed and bit into him. Aden shut his eyes tightly in denial. *Not again. This can't happen again!* A voice suddenly rose above his wild and panicked mind. A different memory that gave him a sliver of hope.

"There will be a time when you'll want, or need, to use your power without focusing it from an extension of yourself, or at a distance greater than what feels possible. See it in your mind, feel it with your body and soul. Picture it. Believe it! Will it to be done!"

They were the words Khodi had told him during one of their many training practices. He'd never been able to command gritt as his friend had. But now he needed to. He wanted to. He had to! His fate was sealed, whichever way this turned out, and he refused to watch helplessly as another friend died. Aden was beginning to feel weak and light-headed from the little air he squeezed into his lungs, but he forced his mind to focus. He buried the fear and panic that tried to overcome him.

Thank you, Khodi.

He focused his attention solely on the deed.

Fraf.... Please... please.... You can't.... Don't die. Don't die!

The rope vanished, and Aden fell.

EPILOGUE

Frafnar's breath caught in between beats of his heart. In utter disbelief, he watched as the weapon shifted in the air and plunged into one of the orcs holding him. Frafnar caught a glimpse of Aden's face and saw the relief before it fell out of sight. His friend was gone.

Quivering with rage, Frafnar's body acted on its own as he pulled himself free of the orc that still held him. He knelt to grab his sword from the ground and made a vertical sweep at the unguarded orc to his side. The crimson was quick enough to step back and avoid the cut, but before he could return the like, Frafnar was already charging toward Garret.

Ohn'na released a force of energy and pushed away all around her. Most of the renegades were flung over the steep edge of the stairs. She focused on the orcs, who had only been uprooted a couple feet, their natural resistance to magic absorbing the blast. Ohn'na was hard-pressed to contend with the three orcs simultaneously, but Frafnar relied on her savvy sword techniques to handle them.

One of Garret's men intercepted Frafnar before he reached his target. Frafnar fell back from a fierce display of swordsmanship, and then smirked when his attacker pounced on his deceptively vulnerable situation. Using the man's momentum against him, Frafnar lifted his foot and threw his overly eager attacker over the incline. To Frafnar's surprise, there was no scream, so he peered over the ledge. The man had used a rare levitation scroll and was slowly descending to the ground. Frafnar hustled to his feet, but Garret used the opening to kick him from behind, sending him over the edge. Unwilling to meet this fate alone, Frafnar used magic to pull Garret over as well.

The descending man got a shock when his weight tripled, with Frafnar and his leader hanging on in succession. The spell wasn't strong enough for such weight, and the descent grew rapid and dangerous. It wasn't until they were about halfway to the ground that the man decided that his life was worth more than his leader's, and kicked and flailed to try and dislodge them. Frafnar held a firm grip while he tried to get rid of his own burden. Garret lost his hold and fell. They were still very high, but Frafnar hoped that Garret would survive so he could be the one to finish him. Frafnar hung on as his lifeline continued to try to free himself. They'd reached the treetops when the man decided he'd try a fireball. Frafnar noticed the fire forming and let go. The man jerked upward from the sudden loss of weight, but looked down to see fire encompass *his* vision.

Frafnar used his power and cushioned most of his fall; only his bones rattled as he landed. Steam rose from his hands as he watched the man fall, leaving a trail of smoke in his wake. It took the knight a moment to gather himself, then he ran in the direction where Garret had landed.

Garret hadn't fared so well. His leg was evidently broken, so he was unable to flee. Instead, the traitor sent bolt after bolt of tainted lightning toward him. At first, Frafnar jumped and dodged behind obstacles, but after a time his patience wore thin and he rushed in and held his blade at Garret's throat.

"You know I am right!" Garret gasped while he tried to drag himself away. "You see, don't you? The Order is weak. They wouldn't save your friend, as they would not me. Something else needs to take their place, someone else."

Frafnar said nothing, but hesitated.

"You could join me, you know," Garret continued, obviously bolstered by Frafnar's pause. "Together we could fix this broken world. Help the crimson—"

Frafnar separated the neck from the body. "There will be no mistakes this time. Let the records show that you are truly dead." He left the worthless carcass to rot and disappeared into the fog.

There had been no sign of Aden, and only his sword remained. The weapon's brilliance was now faded and dull, as if mourning the death of its master. It was proof Aden was truly gone. Ohn'na sat with Frafnar on the edge where their friend had fallen. Her robes had seen better days, with less blood, sweat, and tearstains. The guardian had healed her minor wounds, and none of her injuries were severe. The two knights sat in silence. They could not sense Aden any longer, not a trace.

After a time, Ohn'na put a hand on Frafnar's shoulder. "We should go. We need to inform the keepers what happened here."

Frafnar watched the sunset as Ohn'na limped away. His gaze fell to the sword he held, Aden's weapon. Garret's blade lay nearby; Ohn'na had forgotten to take it with her. They were to return it to the fires, as was tradition. On impulse, Frafnar grabbed the vulgar sword and threw it as hard as he could. *He killed a fellow knight and countless others. He doesn't deserve the honor.*

Frafnar turned his back as the blade tumbled to the ground below. He held Aden's with care and placed it on his belt and faced the fading light one last time. His hand brushed against his familiar companion of disguise. He took the mask off his belt and held it, then put it in its proper place. *The orcs will pay for this, for everything.* As Frafnar finished the thought, the sun slid fully behind the horizon and cast him in shadows.

The body fell through the portal faster than the Slaver had expected, hitting the floor hard. There was a sickening snap, and he cursed. He knew the maneuver had been risky, and now he was certain a bone had broken. He'd be sure to get his compensation later.

Despite the injury, the body didn't stir. To the benefit of all, he lay unconscious. The portal that had been conjured on the ceiling had collapsed and closed moments after the body had fallen through. The room was dark, except for a few candles that basked the room in a soft, warm glow.

"Check him."

Another figure moved immediately to the body and did a thorough examination. "He has a broken arm, but otherwise is unharmed. It should heal without any problems... maybe a month or two."

The Slaver rubbed his chin and relaxed slightly. "Just make sure it heals perfectly; we have all the time in the world now."

That is, until the client's patience runs out. A shiver ran up his spine at the thought of the consequences if that were to happen. He had a feeling his imagination wasn't nearly as horrible as what he'd truly face. Despite that, a smirk formed on his lips while he watched them carry away the body. In this line of work, the hazards could be fatal. But for what he was being paid, it was well worth the risk. He followed his men, to begin building his collection once again.

J.A. ALEXSOO

BLOOD BRANDED

BOOK ONE OF
THE MIX-BLOOD
SERIES

AUTHOR'S NOTE

Thank you so much for your interest in *The Knight's Order*. I would love to know your thoughts, your hopes for future books, any needed improvements, and what characters you liked best. Consider leaving a brief review on Amazon, Goodreads, or on your website. You can also contact me at jaalexsoo.com.

I consider all feedback so please don't be shy. Your opinion matters!

I have read many different genres, but always return to my treasured fantasy novels. When I wrote the first chapter, back in 2010, I never expected it to become a novel. I created a world where the arcane arts weren't feared, and a common occurrence in everyday life. A story about knights and adventure in my own realm. And so, Mythreth and the Avant Guard were born. Knights that were special because they could control magic itself. This novel has changed substantially from my first draft, but I think it has evolved into a thrilling tale.

In 2010, I graduated from university and went to college. I

continued to write through the years. It wasn't until I was in my last year of school that I yearned to escape science and cater to my artistic side. In 2014, I decided to finally write a book. I had been working on a children's picture story at the time, but put that aside to focus on the chapters of my fantasy world. It didn't turn out to be as easy as I thought. In the meantime, I also submitted a short story to Reader's Digest Canada. They chose to publish A Gift Without Wrapping in their 2015 December/January issue. That helped to lift my spirits considerably.

Now, the book is complete and published. It has been a long journey, but I'm excited about the future. I'm working on more books, and I hope, dear reader, you are looking forward to it. If you would like to know how the work is progressing, you can visit jaalexsoo.com and sign up for my newsletter. I hope to meet you there, and I look forward to your feedback!

ACKNOWLEDGMENTS

I couldn't have done this alone. I am so grateful for the expertise, time, energy, and ideas that were contributed to make it the wondrous novel it is.

I want to thank my family, because this was only made possible with your continuous support, motivations, and encouragements. A special thanks goes to Grace, who shared many long nights with me. I could always depend on your honest opinion, and valued your thoughtful insights. I also want to thank Jason, because with your love and understanding, I was able to pursue my dreams. My thanks to Jenn, for her astute remarks despite her many new responsibilities. And my thanks to Wendy for the positive reinforcement which provided the drive I needed to continue on.

A lot has changed in the past few years since I wrote the first chapter, and undoubtedly for the better. This novel wouldn't have reached the quality it has without the work of my editor, David Antrobus, who showed tremendous patience toward my limited writing experience. I appreciated the informative resources and your bright humor.

I would never have had such a professionally illustrated cover if it wasn't for Hugh Pindur. His exceptional skills in graphic design blew me away. Thanks Hugh, it looks awesome!

I was surprised to learn that the interior design of a novel is more involved than I expected. My thanks to Ali Cross for making the inside a work of art for its first printing run.

Last, but definitely not least, thank you dear readers! The adventures in Mythreth couldn't continue without you.

ABOUT THE AUTHOR

J.A. Alexsoo lives in Ontario, Canada, and has forever been a fan of fantasy and science fiction. When not working on writing or imagining new adventures, she tours the lands with her two trusty canine companions.

For exclusive content, visit:
www.JAAlexsoo.com

GLOSSARY

amass stone—The largest stone of its kind, virtually unmovable. Commonly used by keepers to contact other citadels across the world.

aphix stone—Smooth, generally fist-sized stones infused with rune magic to allow users with other stones to communicate over long distances. Commonly used within citadels to communicate.

(the) Avant Guard—An order of talented knights who keep peace in the realms. Also known as the Order. Some call them Ordained.

corves—A species similar to crows in appearance, but much larger. They are commonly used as mounts by Remnents and summoned from another lower realm.

(the) Council—A group of keepers who lead their assigned citadel. Usually only three keepers make up the Council in each citadel.

demose—Demons who fight for domination of Mythreth, commonly using mortals to get a foothold into it. They are attracted to power and revel in death and destruction. They each have their own desires and will destroy other demose if they get in the way of their plans. When they succeed to merge with the mortals of Mythreth, their consciousness takes over.

(the) Divine—A being which is believed to have created all of Mythreth and beyond.

draquor—An ancient species that was experimented on by Remnents.

druids—An elusive race who look human but live longer and never appear to physically age past thirty seasons. They have an affinity for magic, and some believe humans gained the ability to use magic from the mixing of bloodlines. They are gifted with a natural ability to change form into other creatures through will alone.

dwarves—A people who prefer to live and work with stone. They do not embrace magic, avoiding it whenever possible. Despite their disapproval of the arcane, they often work with creatures such as titans and use enchanted items.

(the) Enclave—Northern regions ruled by the Remnents.

exten stone—Similar to the aphix stone, but larger and very difficult to move. Commonly used to send messages to knights out on missions.

goblins—A race that can change their appearance. They are the mortal enemies of the druids.

gritt—Also known as willful magic. A talent which has the power to manipulate and control other magic. All members of the Avant Guard have this ability, at different skill levels. Remnents are also known to have this ability.

guardian—An honorary title given to a knight for a heroic deed or exceptional prowess.

high time—A term meaning noon, when the sun is at its highest. Midday is a variation of this term.

keeper—A member of the Order that resides on the Council that manages a citadel.

kit—Also known as a knight in training, or trainee, in the Avant Guard. A recruit becomes a kit when assigned to learn from a knight.

knight—A member of the Avant Guard that is proficient in weapon combat and magic.

magister—A member of the leading Council of the Avant Guard.

mix-blood—Those whose heritage is of more than one race.

Mythreth—A realm of mortals, neutral ground that the demose try to conquer.

orcs—They are the descendants of ancient humans who revered the demose. These humans relied on the demose for so long that it permanently changed their physical appearance. Eventually their descendants were immune to the coercion and could no longer merge with demons. They remain larger and stronger than their modern human counterpart and have a high resistance to magic.

(the) purging—The act of separating a demon from its host.

recruit—A person who joins the Avant Guard to learn how to control their abilities. They are not promoted to kit unless assigned to a knight.

Remnents—People with gritt who surrender to the demose.

renegades—A person who didn't make it into the Avant Guard and use their abilities to harm others or the Order.

tamed lands—Land that is well populated and regularly traveled through.

titans—beings of energy that merge with matter to take form in Mythreth (Rock, Fire, Water, Wind). Rock titans were the first, then the Fires sparked into being and fought the Rocks for dominance. Water and Fire titans arrived in Mythreth with the dragons that came from another realm.

transpo spell—Magic that instantly teleports the caster a short distance.

verge stone—A stone similar to aphix stones, but smaller and more portable. Used frequently by the Avant Guard, and Remnents. The range of its power is limited, commonly used by knights to communicate with one another when on missions.

wild lands—Land that is dangerous and not extensively explored. There are few detailed maps of the region.

willful magic—Also known as gritt. The ability to manipulate and control other magic.

wyvernkin—A species similar to the dragons known to mortals, but usually smaller and simple-minded. They are not native to Mythreth and are summoned from another realm by the Avant Guard for the purpose of swift travel.